ISBN 978-1-332-06959-0
PIBN 10279961

1 MONTH OF
FREE
READING

at
www.ForgottenBooks.com

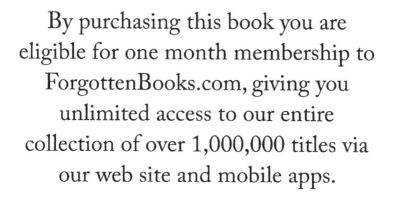

By purchasing this book you are eligible for one month membership to ForgottenBooks.com, giving you unlimited access to our entire collection of over 1,000,000 titles via our web site and mobile apps.

To claim your free month visit:
www.forgottenbooks.com/free279961

English
Français
Deutsche
Italiano
Español
Português

www.forgottenbooks.com

Mythology Photography **Fiction**
Fishing Christianity **Art** Cooking
Essays Buddhism Freemasonry
Medicine **Biology** Music **Ancient
Egypt** Evolution Carpentry Physics
Dance Geology **Mathematics** Fitness
Shakespeare **Folklore** Yoga Marketing
Confidence Immortality Biographies
Poetry **Psychology** Witchcraft
Electronics Chemistry History **Law**
Accounting **Philosophy** Anthropology
Alchemy Drama Quantum Mechanics
Atheism Sexual Health **Ancient History**
Entrepreneurship Languages Sport
Paleontology Needlework Islam
Metaphysics Investment Archaeology
Parenting Statistics Criminology
Motivational

JOB SWEETY "NOBBLING" SUNSHINE.

STABLE SECRETS;

OR,

𝕻𝖚𝖋𝖋𝖞 𝕯𝖔𝖉𝖉𝖑𝖊𝖘.

HIS SAYINGS AND SYMPATHIES.

BY

JOHN MILLS.

AUTHOR OF "THE OLD ENGLISH GENTLEMAN," "THE LIFE OF A RACEHORSE," "THE
FLYERS OF THE HUNT," "THE LIFE OF A FOXHOUND," ETC. ETC.

LONDON:

WARD AND LOCK, 158 FLEET STREET.

1863.

PRINTED BY
PETTER AND GALPIN, BELLE SAUVAGE WORKS,
LUDGATE HILL, E.C.

STABLE SECRETS.

CHAPTER I.

Upon Puffy. Doddles taking his departure for "The Great Stable of the North," his worldly goods, coming under the head of "luggage," were easily confined within the limits of a small blue and white spotted cotton handkerchief, which, suspended on the crooked end of a straight stick, swung easily over his dexter shoulder. Without any decided exhibition of poetical sentiment being expressed on the part of his equals, either jointly or severally, or any marked emotion exhibited from his superior, Mr. Robert Top, Puffy bade a friendly farewell to the former; and a respectful one to the latter, as he turned upon his heel to quit the scene of his early stable days, and the latch clinking harshly, as the great yard gate slowly swung and closed upon its hinges, seemed to cut him off for ever from the inner world.

With much greater ease than he would have been disposed to confess, Puffy Doddles could have wept like a child of tender years; but putting a powerful check upon his inclination, he quitted the spot with a far more dignified effect of grief.

"I shall miss 'm," whispered he, dolefully, to himself; "but I wonder whether they 'll miss me?" and then, in the firm belief that the bottom of the stable pail, on which he had passed so many hours of his life in the saddle-room, or his empty seat in the refectory, wherein he had practised so much self-denial in the reduction of his fat, could scarcely fail to draw kindly thoughts of him when far away, Puffy Doddles felt slightly consoled with the reflection, and, with a lighter heart and lighter step, strode along with his luggage.

The Great Stable of the North was a long way off; but time and distance having—to apply a familiar figurative expression of the head of the family of the Tops—"their heads licked off by steam," Puffy Doddles, after travelling a succession of miles, and scores of miles, above the ground, and under the ground, and through the ground, and between the ground, found himself, in the fulness of time, at the end of his journey, as safe and sound as a crate of crockery, which had been strictly preserved in accordance with the express directions on the label—"This side up with care."

As the Great Stable of the North "loomed in the distance," Puffy Doddles bent a steadfast gaze upon its walls, and stood for a few seconds on a slight eminence with the contemplative air of a pilgrim with the sought-for shrine of his pilgrimage in view.

"That's it, is it?" said he, with a long-drawn sigh. "*That's* the Great Stable o' the North!" and then Puffy Doddles felt a thousand associations flit through his brain connected with that popular institution, and could scarcely get rid of the fear but that he should wake suddenly from a dream too pleasant to be real.

Modesty is ascribed to be an unexceptionable attribute of merit, and, therefore, in stating that Puffy Doddles gave a modest pull at the handle of a bell within easy reach, and, without waiting to be interrogated by the smiling, rosy-cheeked, matronly-looking dame answering the summons, announced his Christian and surname, where he came from, and the immediate object of his then personal attendance at the residence of the chief of the Great Stable of the North in a manner anything the opposite of forward or bold, but governed by a strict sense of the nicest propriety, nothing more than common justice is done to his own personal introduction.

" Walk in, Puffy Doddles," responded the smiling, rosy-cheeked, matronly-looking dame, answering the summons; and, feeling himself quite up to the mark in being able to conform to the request, without altercation or impediment, Puffy Doddles did as he was requested, and, accordingly, walked in.

"The master will be here presently," said the matronly-looking dame, in a combined tone and manner which may fairly be described as pleasant in the extreme. "Sit ye down, my lad."

Obeying the instructions with an abrupt movement, Puffy Doddles dropped upon the surface of a chair, and being forthwith left alone in the apartment into which he had been ushered, began to while away the moments as they flew by, surveying some of the contents therein.

The mirror-like polish of the dark mahogany table standing directly before him reflected his countenance to the particular of a minute pimple on his nose, and presented presumptive evidence that the housewife of the establishment maintained a strong opinion about polish, which the legs and backs of the chairs fully corroborated. Then the numerous portraits of racehorses, suspended in neatly-gilt frames, protected from dust and the trespassing of flies through the transparent medium of muslin, proved that the table and chairs possessed no monopoly in the care bestowed upon them or their polish. But that which drew the particular attention of Puffy Doddles, and fixed his eyes in a way commonly called "riveted," was a jockey's black silk jacket, with yellow sleeves and cap, placed under a glass shade in the centre of the dark mahogany table, with a card on which was written, "The Great St. Leger, 185—."

As if fascinated by the object upon which he gazed, Puffy Doddles continued to examine the colours under the glass shade with a depth of interest scarcely fathomable, and learning their history from the few brief words referring to the particular

event with which they were unquestionably associated, he drew
a long breath, bearing close affinity to a sigh, and exclaimed, in
a much louder tone than he was even conscious of himself, "I
wonder if *I* shall ever have a mount for a Great St. Leger!"

"That 'll a good deal depend upon yourself, my lad," returned a voice; and upon Puffy Doddles turning quickly, with
great confusion of manner, to the quarter whence it came, he
perceived that a stranger stood within a few inches of his elbow.

Puffy Doddles was upon his feet in as short a space of time
as the movement permitted, and created a first favourable
impression upon the stranger by making a respectful, if not a
polite, bow in acknowledgment of his presence.

"That 'll a good deal depend upon yourself, my lad," repeated the stranger, occupying a seat. "But not altogether so,"
added he, measuring Puffy Doddles with a look which, beginning deliberately at his heels, ended somewhere about the
back part of his neck.

A pause ensuing at this juncture, which Puffy Doddles
felt to be almost painful, he ventured to break the monotony
of the reigning silence by remarking that "he was only a-talk-
ing to himself."

"Better that, lad, than a worse companion," rejoined the
stranger. "You know who *I* am?" he added, interrogatively.

"My new master, I—I—I suppose, sir," responded Puffy
Doddles, with a hesitating, deferential air; "Mr. James Sloper."

"Right," returned Mr. James Sloper, with an approving
nod of the head. "We seem to know quite enough about each
other at present. Go out of that door," continued he, pointing
to the only one by which either ingress or egress could be made
to the apartment, "turn to the right, then twice short to the
left, and you'll find yourself near enough to the saddle-room to
ask for the head lad, George Spindles. He will give you orders
what you are to do, and"—here Mr. James Sloper raised a
straightforward forefinger, by way of telegraphing more than
ordinary attention to the concluding part of the sentence he

clearly was, on the point of delivering—"and inform you of a few things you are *not* to do."

"Thank you, sir," returned Puffy Doddles; "I shall pay partickler attention."

"No tricks with 'osses, recollect."

Puffy Doddles earnestly declared "that such a wickedness had never entered his thoughts since the hour of his birth, which he had been led to believe took place over a stable fifteen year' ago come next Lady-day."

"No scamping with your fellow lads," continued Mr. James Sloper, without noticing the evidently honest protestation of innocence in reference to the introductory caution.

Puffy Doddles expressed a constitutional aversion to "scamping."

"No shirking o' your work," resumed Mr. James Sloper, with a demeanour approaching the austere.

Puffy Doddles "could hardly expect, perhaps, to be believed; but still truth *was* truth, and he could look anybody in the face and say he loved his work better than his play."

A smile, expressive of some amount of incredulity upon this point, spread itself over the wan features of Mr. James Sloper, and entertaining the fear, perhaps, that the very favourable account given by Puffy Doddles of himself might reach a fabulous extreme if continued, he conveyed his desire, by a significant movement of a hand, that the interview should terminate at this period of their acquaintanceship, and waved him from the room.

As one of the principal actors in the scenes associated with the sayings and doings of Puffy Doddles, his new master shall now be sketched as he stood, apparently listening to the footfall, gradually becoming indistinct, of the young additional retainer to the Great Stable of the North, on his way to a preliminary interview with the head lad of that establishment, George Spindles.

Mr. James Sloper measured five feet eight inches and a half

in his shoes, and, it may seem unnecessary to add, failed to come up to that exact height when standing simply in his stockings. To borrow a conventional phrase, Mr. James Sloper had seen fifty-eight summers, and consequently must have witnessed about an equal number of winters, although they might not exactly agree to one, more or less. Vigorous and active, both mentally and physically, was Mr. James Sloper; and his pale and deeply-lined countenance bore ample testimony that the summers and winters, to which reference has been made, had not been recorded with the seasons of the past without his having a full share of anxiety in weathering those storms so unerring in their influence upon the barometer of life. Thin, even to bony, was the figure of Mr. James Sloper, and an air of quiet respectability pervaded the long-skirted brown coat, almost dusting his heels as he walked; silver drab gaiters and knee-breeches, waistcoat designed to match in texture and style, and a white cravat, tied with great precision, so as to offer no impediment to a flowing and crimped shirt frill, gave a tone, so to speak, to the general effect, which a white cravat could only have given. As a man of the world—who of the world was most decidedly worldly—Mr. James Sloper knew the marketable value of effect, and paid strict attention to the proper cause for producing it.

A physiognomist of no great pretensions, perhaps, might have formed the hasty conclusion that the expression of Mr. James Sloper's features was that of goodwill and charity with all men; but no greater physiognomical mistake could possibly have been committed. He smiled, it is true, upon most, if not upon all, occasions; but universal benevolence was anything but a deeply planted sentiment in the breast of Mr. James Sloper. In his reflective moments, at an early period of his public life, as a public man in a public stable, he arrived at the irrevocable decision that the duty he owed himself—apart from any claim which society might have upon him, and which he thought expedient to repudiate—was " to get as much money as fast as he could, and keep as much as could possibly be got." Being guided by this comprehensive · principle throughout his adventurous public career as a public man in a public stable, Mr. James Sloper found himself, now that his hair was thin and white, and his eyesight demanded the aid of spectacles, in a fair position to be called rich, and with a strong inclination, strongly developed, to become considerably richer.

The means by which the end was accomplished were—"Stable Secrets."

CHAPTER II.

NOTHING could be more positive, in the shape of a foregone conclusion, than the directions given by Mr. James Sloper, that the interview between George Spindles and Puffy Doddles should be carried out with the utmost precision; and consequently these hitherto personal strangers to each other quickly found themselves in that common position known as "face to face."

"Ho!" exclaimed the head lad of the Great Stable of the North, imitating his master's searching style of receiving Puffy Doddles, by "running his eye over him." "Ho!" repeated he, "you're he, are ye?"

Puffy Doddles intimated that the conjecture was correct in his being the identical he, and no counterfeit.

"Old Robert's best boy, eh?" resumed the interrogator.

Puffy Doddles always did the best he knew how; but that was as much as he could say about himself.

"And quite enough, too," rejoined George Spindles, sententiously. "Can't say too little about oneself. None but a-nass speaks much about hisself. Step in, and let's finish your portrait."

Luckily for the future peace of mind of Puffy Doddles, he refrained from yielding to an impulse, and making a request that his likeness should not be drawn until he had had the opportunity of getting himself up for so express an occasion, as he subsequently learned that "finishing your portrait," in the idiom of George Spindles, signified an ideal sketch, and bore no reference whatever to the limner's art.

"Step in, and let's finish your portrait," reiterated George Spindles, leading the way into what Puffy Doddles knew, at a glance, to be the saddle-room of the Great Stable of the North.

Bridles, bits, girths, reins, saddles, surcingles, hoods, quarter-cloths, breast-pieces, rollers, knee-caps, whips, and spurs, hung in profusion around the walls, exhibiting, at the same time, the perfection of neatness and order in their arrangement. Several coloured prints of " horses saddling *for* the post," " horses going *to* the post," " horses starting *from* the post," " horses winning *on* the post," and other varieties of the same subject, in which " horses and the post " formed the leading features in the several designs, relieved the saddle-room from a general effect which, otherwise, might have been monotonous in the extreme. A small looking-glass suspended over the mantelshelf, upon the surface of which the features of George Spindles were often reflected, to the infinite gratification of their proprietor, might also be classed among its decorative furniture.

" You're turned out of right good hands," observed the head lad of the Great Stable of the North, occupying a chair, and stretching out his legs so that they rested only on the heels of his boots ; " you're turned out of right good hands," repeated he, as he once more " ran his eye over " Puffy Doddles. " I," continued George Spindles, " was once under old Turnip-Tops."

" Were you, indeed, sir ? " almost gasped Puffy Doddles with astonishment.

" Indeed I were," returned the head lad of the Great Stable of the North. " It's many a long year ago," continued he ; " but I've had but two places—there and here."

" And you riz to be what you are ! " remarked Puffy Doddles, with profound admiration of the architect of such an elevated position.

"Yes," resumed George Spindles, pressing his lips together, "I've done myself credit so far; 'but"—and here the speaker drew his legs up spasmodically—"if I could only have stopped short in my growth, and kept my fat down, I should have been a good deal higher. The best mounts in the kingdom would have been mine."

"Would they really, sir?" returned Puffy Doddles, in a tone and manner combining great commiseration. "I began to be seized," continued he, "just in the same way, getting, as Mr. Top said, fatter and fatterer every day; but physic, work, and starvation soon cured me."

"What's your weight?" abruptly asked George Spindles.

"In my shirt," replied Puffy Doddles, "five-stun-nine."

"Keep that dark for the present," added the head lad of the Great Stable of the North, with knitted brow and a look of authority. "Keep that dark, I say, for the present," repeated he.

Puffy Doddles promptly declared that, "if his own mother were alive, she should not be made acquainted with his weight, even if she went down on her bless-ed knees to obtain the information."

"You've heard, I s'pose," said George Spindles, "that when there's no hanky-panky going on, the secret of a race lies in the weights and scales."

Puffy Doddles had heard as much.

"Then keep your own weight dark for the present," reiterated George Spindles, with great sternness of tone and manner combined with mystery.

A most emphatic promise being given that these instructions should be observed to the strict letter of their true intent and meaning, the head lad of the Great Stable of the North appeared satisfied upon the point, and the subject dropped by mutual consent.

A more fitting opportunity, perhaps, may not present itself than now for photographing the external appearance of George Spindles.

As second in command in the Great Stable of the North, he possessed, by right of his position in the social scale, the unquestionable title of "head lad," although no doubt could possibly exist that an interval of many years had elapsed since he possessed the common and too generally disagreeable attributes of boyhood. George Spindles, upon the anniversary of his last natal day, announced that "thirty-eight Legers had been run since he was dropped;" and, admitting this data to be correct, no better circumstantial link could be desired in support of the plain inference that if a lad, in the ordinary acceptation of the term, George Spindles must be an old lad. Greatly to his own mortification, and the detriment of his worldly prospects, George Spindles grew, in spite of every check and artifice known to prevent the gradual increase and expansion of his physical proportions, to a length, width, and weight which effectually stopped him from following the ambitious career of a jockey; and making, as far as it was possible, a virtue of necessity, George Spindles called his philosophy to aid in the praiseworthy attempt to be at length contented with his position, meritoriously attained, as head lad to the Great Stable of the North.

The average strength of his character will be learned hereafter; but among the weak points which belonged to it may be classed extreme personal vanity. In an adverse moment of his fate, George Spindles summed up the several points of his form and face, and the grand total of "a good-looking feller" was forthwith figured on the slate of his memory, never to be rubbed out. And yet, had he seen himself as others beheld him, the probability is that this grand total would have been arithmetically worked more than once. From a complete absence of whisker and all perceptible trace of beard, George Spindles was necessarily barefaced, although never exhibiting, on any recorded occasion, more than that fair amount of assurance attendant on self-respect. "A party," on the eve of borrowing five shillings of George Spindles, was heard to describe his hair as the colour of "a bright chestnut.". The same "party," having borrowed the five shillings of George Spindles and failed to return the loan at the appointed time, was heard to call it "carrots." This great discrepancy, therefore, leaves the historian no certain clue as to the particular shade of the hair of the head lad of the Great Stable of the North. That his eyes were light and grey, and took opposite directions in being brought to bear upon the same object, so as to give him the appearance of circumventing remote corners, no two antagonistic opinions prevailed. That his nose seemed designed exclusively for useful purposes, being devoid of that ornamental part known as "the bridge,", was conceded by the universal voice of everybody; and a corresponding theory met with unanimous support, from the same quarters, concerning the form of his mouth, which, if chiselled at all, must have been chiselled by a very large tool. That his body was long, and supported by thin, short legs, in the shape of a parenthesis, no one ventured to dispute; and that his feet were large and toes square might be proved beyond the possibility of cavil by having recourse to the simple method of "seeing," which insured, as a matter of course, "believing."

And yet the grand total of "a good-looking feller" was figured on the slate of George Spindles' memory, never to be rubbed out.

In "getting himself up," as the head lad of the Great Stable of the North designated making his toilet, originality and care were blended in equal proportions. Entertaining a shrewd notion about "the respectability of a black coat and a white choker," George Spindles seldom presented himself to public gaze in any other established mode of dress. The "choker," from its stiff, unyielding shape, seemed, indeed, modelled from that instrument of capital punishment known as the garotte, and gave the wearer an appearance of being capable of looking over it only while standing on his toes. A waistcoat, of great length, matched the coat in shade and texture, and trousers as tight as trousers could be made so as to hold safely together, through the agency of buttons and stitches, associated his legs with the familiar effect of a couple of sticks of black sealing-wax. It might not have been a perfect circle, but the narrow rim of George Spindles' hat could scarcely have been far removed from a single curved line, every part of which was equally distant from its centre, and lent the wearer a jaunty air, which a Quaker's broadbrim, or looped-up bishop's, would have signally failed in securing.

Such was the attire of George Spindles, when before the footlights of the world's stage, varied by a flexible blue cloth cap, and long-waisted, single-breasted, holland jacket, when occupied behind the scenes of the ancient exhibition, combining the entire business of tragedy, comedy, and farce.

"I needn't waste wind," said the head lad of the Great Stable of the North, "in telling ye what you know already."

Puffy Doddles agreed in the self-evident absurdity of adopting an opposite course.

"Just so," continued George Spindles. "Then all I shall say is, if you are to get on in this shop, you must never want to be told twice about anything, whether it's to be done or undone."

Puffy Doddles could not recollect a single instance of his life when instructions, once given, had to be repeated.

"Very good," resumed George Spindles, "then don't begin to have 'em cuckoo'd just now. As to stable dooties, you know all about them," continued he; "old Turnip-Tops put you through that sieve well, I know. But remember night and day, sleeping and waking, eating, drinking, and even when shaving, that you are *now* in the Great Stable of the North! Look sharp, hear sharp, think sharp, but"—the speaker paused, and bringing his lips close to his ready listener's nearest ear, whispered—"be as mute as if you were in the mole country," and jerking the point of a finger towards the ground immediately beneath his feet, conveyed his meaning of the "mole country" with considerable illustrative power.

"Almost Mr. Top's very own words, sir," observed Puffy Doddles, smiling at the reminiscence.

"Ah!" rejoined George Spindles, screwing up one of his eyes, in order to get, perhaps, a concentrated aim with the other, "the old buffer has been in the swim himself, and knows his way about! But come," continued he, rising from his seat, "and I'll show you the colt you're to look after."

Puffy Doddles expressed the utmost willingness to conform with this request, and following his mentor to a long row of boxes, flanking one side of a brightly-gravelled, well-kept stable-yard, entered a door, by the express invitation of George Spindles, and was informed that before him stood "the best two-year-old out"—SUNSHINE.

CHAPTER III.

FROM the antecedents of Puffy Doddles it may be inferred that he was not an accomplished professor of the art coming under the head of "chaffing," and, although much practised in the society in which he moved, from the early stages of life to the present epoch, no perceptible progress was made even in the rudiments of the science. As a complete novice, therefore, Robert Top's "best lad" found himself greatly exposed to the shafts of satire, winged in flights upon his introduction to the Great Stable of the North, and frequently deemed it expedient to retire rather than face the attack with such unequal odds arrayed against him. One Tom Trigg may be said to have occupied the prominent position of leader to the hostile forces, and the injuries which this enemy to Puffy's peace of mind inflicted were not caused through the agency of

> "A polished razor keen,
> Wounding with a touch, which was scarcely felt or seen."

Mr. Trigg's notions in "coopering up a feller," as he described his visitations of this kind, were more of the crowbar tendency, and, in accomplishing the task, he used the whole of the force of which he felt himself master.

"What's your name?" inquired Tom Trigg, at an early period of their acquaintanceship, and when backed by a strong force of attendant parasites in jackets and gaiters.

"Doddles," replied the new comer, with combined meekness in tone and manner, as he had already told him.

"Is it really!" rejoined Tom Trigg, with feigned astonishment—"Doddles, is it? I've heard that name before."

"No doubt," returned Puffy, with pardonable pride, "for it's always been coupled with 'osses."

"Yes," added Trigg, "and knackers' yards. You may see it once or twice, too," continued he, "in the Newgate Calendar."

Puffy begged to think, with due submission, that his informant was greatly mistaken, or if a Doddles *had* been connected with knackers' yards, or charged with offences of a nature likely to be recorded in the history of crime, the name would be found spelt differently to his, and probably with one *d* only.

The attendant parasites in jackets and gaiters were now indulging in that silent expression of mirth known as "broad grins."

"How's your mother?" abruptly asked Tom Trigg.

Puffy Doddles heaved a gentle sigh, and with a slight shake of the head, scarcely perceptible, announced that his maternal parent no longer belonged to the state terrestrial.

"She was in training, once, wasn't she?" said Mr. Trigg.

"Training!" repeated Puffy Doddles, with mingled indignation and astonishment. "What for?"

"Backed for five monkeys, I was told," returned Tom Trigg.

Again Puffy Doddles requested to be made acquainted with the undertaking or particular event for which his ever anxious mother had been in training.

"To talk a hawse's ed of, I heard," replied Mr. Trigg,

"walk a mile, run a mile, bowl a hoop a mile, eat a leg of mutton, drink a bucket of beer, and give suction to a brace of twins, in thirty minutes fifteen seconds. Latest betting, five to four on the old gal."

The disposition of Puffy Doddles was anything but of a pugnacious character; but upon the unwarrantable introduction of this fictitious match between his kind, old, departed mother, against time, and the deafening applause which followed on the part of the attendant parasites, he was observed to turn up the sleeves of his holland jacket with a deliberate and slow movement, and throwing his cap upon the ground with as gallant a bearing as ever knight of old threw down his steel gauntlet of defiance, proclaimed, in the absence of any herald to perform the office, that he was "then and there ready to take it out of the best man among 'em."

Upon this bold challenge being given, Mr. Tom Trigg became a conspicuous object, upon which the concentrated looks of the attendant parasites in jackets and gaiters were riveted in silence; and it must be confessed that that oracle of wit in the Great Stable of the North presented anything but an appearance of ease as he found himself the centre of attraction of the eyes referred to. A bright red tinge mantled over his cheeks, mounting quickly even to his forehead, and he stammered forth a hesitating, weak, lame, and impotent refusal to run the risk of having it "taken it out of him" just then, on particular grounds, which he thought proper to reserve for the moment as a secret between himself and his conscience.

"Is there anybody else who would like to have it taken out of him?" returned the valiant Puffy, glancing around, and lightly throwing himself in an attitude especially adapted both for offence and defence.

None of the attendant parasites in jackets and gaiters, however, appeared more inclined than their leader to accept the general invitation of "having it taken out of them." One. must "go and look after his 'oss;" another "thought he was called;" a third "believed he was wanted;" but where, by whom, or concerning what, did not appear. A fourth "couldn't stay;" a fifth discovered the immediate necessity of going, and in a few seconds Puffy Doddles, still occupying an attitude especially adapted both for offence and defence, found himself alone, master of the position, without an individual member of the hostile forces in sight. From that moment Robert Top's best lad might date his complete immunity from Mr. Trigg's taunts and sarcasm ; and, if not regarded with absolute fear, he felt that his appeal to physical force had produced an impression closely allied to that respectful feeling.

Puffy Doddles strode from the scene of his triumph with a corresponding confidence of the Third Richard, when he announced unequivocally that "he was himself again."

"I've settled *their* business," said Puffy Doddles, and, as evidence of inward satisfaction at the settlement, forthwith commenced warbling a few lines of that favourite ballad of his :

> " Of all the gals that are so smar-r-rt,
>   There's none like pretty Sally ;
>   She is the darling of my hear-r-rt ;
>   And she lives in our alley."

" Have ye got a lock of her hair ? " interrupted a voice ; and upon turning to the spot whence the interrogatory came, Puffy Doddles perceived the form of George Spindles looming in the perspective. "Have ye got a lock of her hair ?" repeated the head lad of the Great Stable of the North, with the corners of his mouth drawn back, and exhibiting the outward effects of an inward explosion of laughter, unaccompanied by the smallest audible sound.

Puffy Doddles admitted that he did not possess the graceful token of affection from the particular young lady referred to, and that, in fact, she was litttle more than an airy nothing, or a name.

" No Sal in the case, eh ? " rejoined George Spindles.

Puffy Doddles pledged his honour that he never had a relative, connection, friend, or acquaintance, as far as he either knew or believed, of the name of Sally.

"Glad to hear it," returned George Spindles. "We don't want our lads to be soft upon Sallys, or Bettys neither, I can tell ye," continued he. "I knew a bit of muslin once that nearly ruined all Yorkshire."

A bit of muslin nearly ruined all Yorkshire! Puffy Doddles dropped his lower jaw, and raised his eyebrows to their fullest stretch with astonishment.

"*That* bit of muslin," resumed the head lad of the Great Stable of the North, "was a lady's maid of the name of Matilda; and a plump, pretty little black-eyed lass Matilda was. I think I see her now," added George Spindles, folding his arms across his somewhat narrow chest, and casting a look of mingled meditation and regret upon his boots.

"You knew her, then?" remarked Puffy Doddles.

"I knew her well," returned the head lad of the Great Stable of the North, "and a plump, pretty little black-eyed lass Matilda was," repeated he, still keeping a steadfast, thoughtful gaze bent upon his boots.

Puffy Doddles, not knowing what to say during the short awkward pause which now ensued, exercised a wise discretion, perhaps, in saying nothing.

"It happened in this way," resumed George Spindles. "There was a tout of the name of Sweety in these parts once, and he, somehow or other, got round Matilda so as to plant herself upon a certain head lad belonging to a stable no great distance off. Being a little soft, ye see, upon the subject of gals, this head lad dropped into the mischief like a blind puppy rolling over the edge of a ditch. Through a good deal of wheedling and coaxing on her part, Matilda got to know the secrets of the stable, and"—here George Spindles' voice became husky from deep emotion—"she split!"

"What a varmint!" exclaimed Puffy Doddles, incapable

of resisting the impulse of thus expressing his sentiments upon the duplicity of the base Matilda.

"Sweety," continued the head lad of the .Great Stable of the North, "took advantage of her weakness, and for a time played a pretty little game by putting us all in the hole. *I*," said George Spindles, emphatically, "nearly came to grief altogether."

Puffy Doddles felt extremely pleased that his approach to sorrow was not of a closer description, and expressed himself so with the utmost sincerity.

"It's all over now," added the head lad of the Great Stable of the North, with a deeply-drawn sigh; "but it took a long time to get it over, I can tell ye. But come," continued he, with marked alteration in tone and manner, "your 'oss wants looking after. It's feed time."

Puffy Doddles exhibited a prompt inclination to relieve the immediate wants of his horse, whatever they might be, and hastened with a nimble tread towards the box in which stood "the best two-year-old out"—SUNSHINE.

CHAPTER IV.

IT was not an easy seat. The bottom of a stable-pail never was, and never can be made, an easy seat. There is no rest for the vertebræ of the spine for "the forked animal, walking erect and eating cooked viands," when sitting on the bottom of a stable-pail. He has nothing upon which to rest his elbows, excepting the contracted surface of his knees, and these acting as points against points, geometrically described as parts without magnitude, render the angle to be of the most acute form, not to say slippery. There is barely sufficient space for· stretching out his legs, from the want of length, breadth, and depth of his common centre—if such it may be called; and, in doubling them up to meet the contingency, he suffers cramp.

And yet, notwithstanding these insurmountable drawbacks to the natural instinct of relaxing the pressure of the thews and sinews, commonly called "taking it easy," Puffy Doddles might frequently be seen seated on the bottom of a stable-pail. Force of habit, perhaps, acted as the "why" for the "wherefore," which lessened the penalties of the position of Puffy Doddles when sitting upon the bottom of a stable-pail; but there, it may be repeated, he frequently sat, reflecting on the past, and contemplating the future.

> "To-morrow, and to-morrow, and to-morrow,
> Creeps in this petty space from day to day."

It seemed, indeed, but yesterday when Robert Top's best lad, acting upon instructions, deftly stripped the neat clothing from Sunshine's shining back and quarters, and revealed to view, for the first time to his new attendant, a form which, taking it all in all, Fate had not awarded him with the opportunity of beholding before, and yet several yesterdays had come and gone since then, to prove that the great total of life "lives in but little."

Puffy Doddles had "looked after" Sunshine for three clear weeks. He had walked, cantered, galloped, and sweated him. He had dressed, fed, and watered him. He had set his box fair daily, even to the particular position of the single, straight, reed-like straws at his heels. He had so polished the bit of his exercising-bridle, suspended on a peg within convenient reach in the box, that it shone like burnished silver. He had systematically cleaned out his crib, so that not the husk of a single oat could be picked out of the smallest crack, corner, or crevice with the point of the finest needle that was ever filed. He had most scrupulously kept from wasting even that limited quantity of hay coming under the definition of a pinch. He had been more punctual in his attendance at the fixed and

stated hours in Sunshine's box than the movements of the best
of parish clocks either would or could have regulated.   To the
moment itself Puffy was there or thereabouts; and as a
summary to what he did and did not, it may be briefly stated
that, far exceeding the reasonable expectations of the chief
of the Great Stable of the North, his several duties were
performed with unprecedented exactness.

Robert Top's best lad, within the small margin of three
weeks since his introduction to the mysteries of that popular
institution, found himself in favour with his superiors and
respected by his equals, to say nothing of his inferiors in the
social scale, who might possibly have had something to say
upon the subject the reverse of complimentary.

Upon the bottom of a stable-pail, up in the morning early,
Puffy Doddles sat, as he had often sat in days gone by.
Before him stood Sunshine, clothed in his box, with one ear
pricked and the other thrown back, as if prepared to receive
prompt intelligence, through the direct medium of acoustics,
from directly opposite points of the compass.   His square-cut
tail, almost as fine as unspun silk, hung motionless and nearly
level with his hocks, and his near hind foot, white as snow
from the coronet to a little above the pastern, rested upon the
extreme point of the toe.   At his most perfect ease, and
indolent as became the leisure moments of "the best two-
year-old out," Sunshine stood in his box, with his punctual
attendant as sole witness of his listlessness.

Puffy Doddles, through the agency of a damped thumb,
was engaged in turning over the leaves of a volume for which
his knees acted as a temporary reading-desk.   Earnestly, and
with a scrutinising look turned upon the contents of each
succeeding page, Robert Top's best lad seemed to be master of
the contents with a concentrated force of which his respective
and collective senses were capable of monopolising.

"Here it is again!" soliloquised he.   "Here it is again!
'Sunshine, by Glitter, dam Comet, by Falling Star.'   Upon my"

—Puffy Doddles hesitated previous to selecting his basis, and then added—"sólemn davy, you're in everything! There's not a stake," continued he, "worth winning, but what you're in. Talk about engagements! why, here they are like strings of sausages, one off and the other on ! May I be hanged"— and then Robert Top's best lad looked as if in his mind's eye he saw at a glance the awful responsibility associated with the hempen twist encircling his throat—"but having the choice, I'd rather not," added he, by way, perhaps, of qualifying the end of his anticipated earthly career—"but- you're in everything. You are, indeed. Here we've got ye in the Newmarket July Stakes, the *Criterion*, the Palatine, the Two Thou', the Derby, the Ascot Derby, the Goodwood Derby, the St. Leger, the Don Stakes, the Select Stakes, and the Stewards' Plate at Winchester ! *And* the Stewards' Plate at Winchester.!" repeated Puffy Doddles, with marked emphasis upon the conjunction. "What next ?" added he, rising from his seat on the bottom of the stable-pail, with a perfect glow of satisfaction, lending a transient effect of redness to his features. "I should like to be informed," continued Puffy Doddles, striding to the near side of Sunshine, "what next ?"

At the conclusion of this query, Sunshine, by Glitter, dam Comet; by Falling Star, lifted the foot—white as snow from the coronet to a little above the pastern—and, with both ears thrown back, threatened to give the questioner a practical retort of considerable force, not to add unanswerable strength.

"Come, come," returned Puffy Doddles, with the utmost confidence that the menace was one of the most transparent shams ever beheld, "none o' your nonsense ! I know all about lashing out. When meant it isn't done in *that* style."

Sunshine felt perhaps that it was useless, after this unqualified avowal, to attempt to practise the deception one moment longer ; for, dropping his foot into the ordinary position of supporting the fair proportion of his weight, and pricking his ears forward, the son of Glitter, and Comet turned his head, and rubbed and nestled his velvety nose among the nicely-starched front of Puffy Doddles' Sunday shirt, greatly to the disarrangement of the careful design of the laundress.

"Roll me over, indeed!" exclaimed Robert Top's best lad, acknowledging Sunshine's caresses by gently chafing his velvety nose with one hand, and smoothing down the bright, glossy, chesnut-coloured neck of "the best two-year-old out" with the other, as it was bent in a graceful arch to meet the tenderness given and returned. "Roll me over, indeed!" repeated Puffy Doddles. "Why, you'd sooner kick yourself out of your skin, and that ye know as well as I do."

Sunshine, perhaps, knew even better than the speaker what his sentiments were upon this particular subject; but he did nothing more than to continue rumpling the folds of the front of Puffy Doddles' Sunday shirt through the agency of gentle friction.

"They say, and this tells me," resumed Robert Top's best lad, touching the volume he had been perusing with so much interest, and which was now thrust into a side-pocket of his Holland jacket—"they say, and this tells me," repeated he, "that you're the best two-year-old out. Your blood, shape, growth, and performances—which are out-an'-out, as nobody can deny—tell me that you're what Mr. Top would call a flyer. You've done all your friends ever asked; and done it well, too, with a little over, which is a good deal more than can be said of any Christian that *I* ever made acquaintance with yet. Such being the case, all you've got to do," continued Puffy Doddles, addressing the object of his regard in a tone and manner which pourtrayed a thorough conviction that he was perfectly understood, "is to go on just as you've began. No improvement is wanted when the work's done as well as it can be done. That having been your little game up to this point, all I ask, now *I'm* looking after ye, is to go in and win while you've got legs to stand on, or a heart to make 'm move."

Sunshine increased the gentle friction against the starched

front of Puffy Doddles' linen until it began to bear the effect of a duster recently employed by an energetic maid-of-all-work.

"In course," continued the exemplary lad lately recommended by the head of the family of the Tops, and described in his letter as his "best"—"in course," repeated he with a sarcastic sneer, "professionals will have the mounts in all these engagements. *I* don't stand a chance of having a leg up. But let 'em look out," added he, with a significant motion of the head. "Let 'em look out. You've a temper of your own, and will show it, perhaps, when least expected. You'll want riding, *you* will; not bullying. I know ye, and, what's better, you know me. Hah! there's more in the 'oss knowing his rider than most folks are aware of. Isn't there, my pink of toolips?"

The pink of tulips increased the friction to an extent which threatened to rub holes of great magnitude in the front of Puffy Doddles' Sunday shirt.

"They'll call ye by-an'-by," resumed the speaker, "a bad-tempered brute—one that can't be depended upon. They'll say you'll race when ye like, and shut up when you don't. They'll be afraid to trust ye, and yet, knowing what you can do, be more afraid *not* to trust ye. I see it all," added the speaker, partly closing his eyes as if to get a stronger focus for looking into the future; "it's all coming. I shall be wanted."

CHAPTER V.

NOBODY in particular, but everybody in general, stated as a great fact, replete with interest of a most absorbing character, that Sunshine had "wintered well." There was no dispute, no shade of difference of opinion, as to the unexceptionable man-ner in which Sunshine, by Glitter, dam Comet, by Falling Star, had wintered. Weather permitting, he had done good and strong work; weather declining, he had borne the interval of ease and recreation without any perceptible detriment to his health. Independent as any horse could possibly be of either the temporary or permanent condition of the weather, Sunshine had gone well, stood still well, eaten well, and, for aught to any appearance to the contrary, slept well. Without even a suspicion of "a screw being loose," for a single moment of the term, the best two-year-old out satisfied his friends and admirers that he had "wintered well;" and more than that, on the part and behalf of this select body, nothing more was either required or expected. When Sunshine's "spring condition" formed the subject of discourse, his "party"—the Northern division—spoke in subdued whispers, exchanged looks significant of being "up to a thing or two," thrust their hands to the bottom of their breeches pockets to jingle loose cash together, and, by way, perhaps, of a little musical variation, began to whistle a few bars of popular airs very much out of tune. This "party"—this Northern division—entertained a strong, not to add forcible idea, that they were the privileged few in comparison to numbers in undisturbed possession of "*the* secrets of the stable." Whether they were so or not, the sequel may possibly reveal.

As a decided opposition, however, to these sanguine supporters and firm believers in the powers and "spring condition" of Sunshine, many shook their heads doubtingly, and in various ways communicated a palpable mistrust of something or somebody, or of relative causes operating between the two somebodies or somethings, possessing equal influence upon the result, and seemed altogether anything but satisfied about that which the "party"—the Northern division—appeared to regard with an unlimited amount of confidence.

"Is he meant?" that was the question. "Can he stay?" *that* was another. "Will he be pulled out for the Two Thou' or kept back for the Derby?" might be added as a third interrogatory combining both general and local interest. "Is the stable money on?" was asked in various dialects in which the

Saxon idiom is used; and "if not on, will it be put on? and if not, how otherwise?"

Many, earnest, and even stern were the several questions put regarding the colt by Glitter, dam Comet, by Falling Star; and, as may be conjectured, many, earnest, and even stern were the several answers given in reply.

The public, as a body, with more heads than brains, announced itself "puzzled." The movements of the Great Stable of the North had been watched, perhaps, by sleepy, heavy-eyed watchmen, who, probably, as an excuse for their drowsiness, frankly avowed that " there was no making out what was meant. If pulled out for the Two Thou', Sunshine must win in a trot; but his stable-companion, Catch-me-who-can, might, after all, be their horse; and if so—well! in *that* case every guinea laid on Sunshine was as good as lost. It was like laying against a dead-'un, and no possible loophole for the admission of a mistake."

Mr. James Sloper smiled a meek, quiet, unpretending smile as the day approached for making known what his decision had long since been with regard to the most profitable tactics for pulling off "the Two Thou'," as Puffy Doddles abbreviated the first great spring prize. To apply a conventional phrase, Mr. James Sloper was a man of very few words. He spoke as little, perhaps, as any one gifted with the ordinary powers of speech; but, like a certain parrot, remarkable for silence, made good the deficiency by the concentrated powers of thought. Had, however, Mr. James Sloper given expression to those reflections upon the subject to which reference is now being made, he probably would have delivered himself something in this style:

"What's the public to me? It doesn't pay training ex's, does it? It doesn't pay entrance money, nor forfeits, nor make good stakes, does it? It doesn't breed, rear, buy, break, nor keep colts or yearlings, does it? It has nothing to do with brood mares, sires, fees, foals, hay, straw, and corn, has it? It doesn't tip for the mounts; concerns itself nothing about

travelling from one part of the kingdom to the other, and yet
expects to see a race-'oss bred, broken, trained, entered, and
brought to the post fit to run on his merits, and win the Bank
of England for the public! When it pulls off a good stake, it
doesn't say, 'Here's a share of what you've done for us,' does it?
And when it loses—no matter how or why—a good deal of
anti-scriptural is indulged in, and the Stable's called a low set
of sanguinary appropriators. A good deal I have to care for
the public! Just about as much as the public has to care for
me." And then Mr. James Sloper might have been seen to
gently rub the ends of his fingers together—as was his wont—
not for the purpose of creating the smallest increase of circulation, but as a cat chafes her nose now and then, as a preliminary, perhaps, to using her claws.

Now it must be conceded as a truism that things may
possess life without being at the same time lively, as the bivalve
oyster, whelk, and other molluscous animals bear ample testimony. The same rule applies to the great consumers of oysters,
whelks, and other molluscs, when a man declares that "he is
more dead than alive," and looks the perfect exemplification of
what he says. There are degrees of life, as there are degrees of
heat and cold, and strength or weakness in foreign spirits, snuff,
tobacco, and British beer. From a pressure of circumstances,
to which it is unnecessary to refer at the present moment, Puffy
Doddles had "many a time and oft," since his introduction to
the Great Stable of the North, felt "more dead than alive,"
although entirely free from the smallest indication that he was
about shaking off this mortal coil.

Alive, but not lively, Robert Top's best lad knew, occasionally, what it was to be a long way off from that circle of
acquaintances with whom he had spent many pleasant evenings
in playing pitch and toss, cribbage, varied by a "go in," now
and then, of odd man. Whatever bitterness, however, was
engendered in comparing the pleasures of the past with the
self-denial and want of joy in the present, Puffy Doddles never

looked more alive, never exhibited a more thorough briskness
of demeanour, than when entering Newmarket by the main
street, for the first time in his life, mounted on Sunshine. The
advent of the horses from the Great Stable of the North invariably caused Newmarket to wake up from that doze which seems
habitual to it. Newmarket, with an effort, threw off dull sloth,
and, rousing itself to action, proceeded to examine the closely-
clothed forms of Sunshine and Catch-me-who-can, as they strode
along with a light and springy tread, " the observed of many
observers." George Spindles, riding the Time Keeper, followed
in the rear ; and as the three pointed their way towards the
stable prepared for their reception, each following within a few
yards of the heels of the other, Newmarket looked on with ill-
concealed sensations of hope, fear, doubt, amity, enmity, and—
taken either together or separately—with heartfelt sentiments
of so opposite a character as to produce the meeting of elements
without possessing the smallest attribute of attraction of cohe-
sion. No mingling, no mixing of feelings, so as to form an har-
monious whole, like, for instance, a bowl of palatable punch,
brewed by the hand of a master of the high art, was manifest
in the outward expression of Newmarket upon the entry of Mr.
James Sloper's horses. The chief of the Great Stable of the
North had both his chosen friends and appreciating admirers in
Newmarket ; but, like public men generally, and particularly
as a public trainer in the greatest of public training stables, Mr.
James Sloper knew, as well as any man living, the great diffi-
culty of pleasing everybody ; and taking advantage of his knowledge, gained by experience, confined his efforts, therefore, to
please the few—that few so limited as to come under the head
of ONE—and that " one " being himself. Newmarket was
acquainted with this piece of private information, as well as
Mr. James Sloper himself ; and, judging of the future by the
past, determined if possible to be governed in its own movements by the causes—either direct or relative—which pulled
the wires of that distinguished man's doings on the coming

event, already casting its trembling shadow upon the threshold
of the present.

The problem to be solved, however, still remained difficult
of solution.   Two horses had arrived from the Great Stable of
the North, both engaged in the Two Thousand Guineas ; both
were supposed good enough to win the stake—both were quoted
in the betting—both were "said to be tried to a pound of being
as good as the other."   Now, as both could not win, and ONE
would only be started, or, at least, "go" for the money, which
was *that* ONE ?   Newmarket shook its head—Newmarket
found itself in a perfect maze, not knowing which way to turn.
Newmarket had its misgivings.   Newmarket screwed its
knuckles into the corner of its eyes, and began to shed tears of
weakness.

There was one, however, who laughed in his sleeve—not an
inhabitant, but a sojourner in Newmarket.   Mr. James Sloper,
as a preliminary to sipping about as nice a glass of claret as
Newmarket could produce, slowly closed one eye—it matters
not which—and rolling the end of his tongue into the corner
of a cheek, held the glass of claret between the pair of transparent wax candles placed upon the table immediàtely before
him, and observed, with an expression of countenance approaching the benevolent, that "it was a deadly game."   Mr. James
Sloper moistened his lips with the wine, and then, continued :
"It puts me in mind," said he, "of thimble-rig.   It does,
indeed.   One, two—here you are, there ye go.   Different
people have 'different opinions—some like happles, some like
hinions.'   Exactly so, *ex*-actly so !" exclaimed he, emptying
the glass to the last drop, and once more filling it, until the
blood-red line encircled the brim, before resuming the gossamer
thread of his thoughts.   "There's no making a certainty of
winning a race," said Mr. James Sloper, with a pleasant smile.
"Accidents bar that.   But "— and here he again had recourse
to the mildly stimulating effects of the claret—" the money laid
against a horse may always be secured when the strings are

pulled by—ha! ha! ha!—by, we'll say, if you please," said Mr. James Sloper, nodding familiarity at vacancy, "the man behind the door, or round the corner, or anywhere except in a conspicuous. place for spectacles to bring him within a short range of the public gaze. Where so much uncertainty *must* exist," resumed the chief of the Great Stable of the North, "what a comfort it is to know that, by a little delicate working of the oracle, a certainty may always be relied upon. When a puny, snivelling, scrubby boy"—and by the familar nod which he gave to mid-air, he seemed to be again addressing a phantom friend—"I was told that *the* secret of life was to play for large gains with small stakes. How much better, therefore, must be that game which insures a good profit without the ghost of a risk! There's no improvement upon a profit without a risk. Hankypanky, and fiddle as ye may, the mind of man can go no further!"

Having arrived at this conclusion, Mr. James Sloper finished his claret, and retired, with a stately tread, to the shades of his dormitory.

Puffy Doddles had long since courted "the sweet repose of Nature's soft nurse," but the soft nurse formed anything but a rightful claimant to the title on this particular occasion. Puffy Doddles tossed about wildly in the confined space allotted him as a shake-down in Sunshine's stable on the night previous to his starting for the great Newmarket Spring event. The legs and arms of Robert Top's best lad whirled round and flew about in a way scarcely capable of description. Large beads of perspiration oozed upon his forehead, and, gathering together, trickled slowly in a continuous stream down his nose. His lips were compressed, and his teeth ground together with a harsh grating noise, not dissimilar to a glazier's diamond cutting through glass.

"Won!" cried he, in a thick husky voice, "won in a walk!"

CHAPTER VI.

In the fulness of time, and long before the early village cock had made his usual matin request for the drowsy milkmaid to "ope-the-dairy-do-or" with all convenient dispatch, Puffy Doddles shook off as feverish a slumber as ever mocked the effects of " Nature's sweet restorer." Robert Top's " best lad " bore the outward appearance of being far removed from the smallest perceptible right to that enviable distinction. He looked, indeed, as having conducted himself in a manner most likely to produce a name anything but the superlative of " good." To allege that Puffy Doddles illustrated that physical and mental condition well-known among "loose fish " as " seedy," barely comes up to the mark of a faithful description of the state of his inward and outward feelings upon the morning of that eventful day when Sunshine was to realise or disappoint the hopes of his " party " for the Two Thousand Guineas ; to say nothing of filling with joy or breaking—in a figurative sense—the sensitive heart of his attendant. The dream, it is true, ended brilliantly, in the son of Glitter and Comet winning in " a walk ;" but Puffy Doddles recollected, the moment he became conscious of being awake, to have heard that visions of the night were governed by laws emanating from adverse causes. If, therefore, his dream was not directed by exceptional influences, " winning in a walk " clearly signified " beaten in a trot." The deduction proved anything but soothing to the already dejected feeling of Puffy Doddles. His breast heaved with a long-drawn sigh, and the air drawn quickly between his tightly-clenched teeth hissed with the sound of an irritated goose.

Robert Top's best lad combed his hair backwards through the medium of his fingers, and, having got it in a bunch from the forehead, held it in a vice-like grasp, as he stared at nothing, although looking into the hazy future with the " mind's eye," which often stretches far beyond the best of telescopes or most powerful of lens.

"Something's up," curtly observed Puffy. "Something's up," repeated he. " I feel it all over, but particularly here," and then, still holding the bunch of hair in a vice-like grasp with one hand, he applied the other, with an affectionate and almost caressing pressure, to just below the waistband of his drab cloth breeches, which had not been removed since his entry into New-market. "Particularly here," reiterated he, again making a temporary indenture with the points of his fingers.

Ay, Puffy Doddles! Stare as you may, stare as you will, stare as you do, the "something up" will beat the entire stock of your philosophy. Bred and born, for aught can be said or written to the contrary, a mathematician of no common order (one, perhaps, who could give the why and wherefore on Related Caustics of reflection, and the Evolute of the Lemniscata, as derived from a caustic of the Hyperbola), still this "something up" shall prove a problem too subtile for that knowledge, either natural or acquired, which you possess of the science treating of magnitude and numbers.

It may be that Puffy Doddles arrived by either a direct or circuitous route at this conclusion ; for, releasing the bunch of hair from between his fingers, he allowed it to take a less con-strained form, and giving himself a shake, not unlike a vigorous spaniel upon emerging from a plunge in a pool, looked, if not quite, yet something like himself again.

" Come what will," said he, striding forwards and lifting the warm rug from Sunshine's glossy quarters, as he gave him his practical morning greeting by the hearty smack of the flattened palm of a hand—" Come what will,"·repeated he, " we'll hope for the best, won't we, old feller ?"

"Old feller" threw back both ears, and lifted the near hind leg in an attitude of the most threatening description.

" That might do well enough for a novice," coolly resumed Sunshine's attendant, "but it won't do for *me;*" and again ad-ministering the practical greeting, dropped the corner of the rug over his sleek quarters, and proceeded to remove that medium of a compulsory abstinence—the "setting muzzle."

"You'd be in a pretty form to be pulled out for the Two Thou', you'd be, if it wasn't for this," remarked Puffy Doddles, releasing the strap which held the instrument like a large leather thimble over Sunshine's jaws and nostrils. "Cut short your 'lowance of hay," continued he, "and ye go to straw as if it was beans. Talk about grubbing, *I* don't believe a greater grubber ever grubbed. I don't, indeed—I don't upon my religious word of honour."

Sunshine, at this particular juncture of the earth's evolution upon her axis, made a playful snap at a certain part of Puffy Doddles' person, which he found well-constituted for sitting upon, and catching a loose or disengaged part of the drab cloth breeches, raised him suddenly, if not gracefully, from the ground. As if conscious, however, of having committed an act of violation of the recognised laws of politeness, the son of Glitter and Comet opened his jaws in that brief space of time known as a twinkling, and dropped his more than a mouthful as if somewhat too hot to hold.

"Come, I say," ejaculated Robert Top's best lad, in a tone and manner scarcely to be called his own; "what are ye up to now? Going to swaller a feller?" inquired he, as he gained his perpendicular, and felt for damages.

Sunshine evinced a prompt admission of having no real intention of swallowing the most exemplary of stable lads, or to injure any part of the raiment which covered him, and conveyed this assurance by rubbing, in a gentle, conciliatory manner, the side of his head against his attendant's shoulder.

"That's all very well, ye know," said Puffy Doddles, soothed, but not perfectly appeased. "That's all very well, ye know," repeated he, still feeling for damages, "but supposin', ye know, you'd—eh?—taken a mouthful. What would there have been left, I should like to know?"

Sunshine, perhaps, had he understood the comprehensive nature of the interrogatory, might have replied, "Take nothing from nothing, and nothing remains." As it was, however, he continued rubbing his head, with a monotonous movement, against the shoulder of Puffy Doddles.

"Come," said Robert Top's best lad, "there's no time to be lost," and divesting himself of one or two superfluous articles of dress, Puffy Doddles stood in the airy costume of a calico shirt and unbraced pair of drab cloth breeches. Then it was that, with a nimble but careful handling, he racked Sunshine's head up, threw his hood lightly, and, with almost a ballet-like movement over his quarters, washed out his mouth with an even six go-downs of water, and presented him with a feed of corn as good as the best granary in Newmarket could produce. Then it was that, after gathering up in a basket what had frequently been gathered before under similar circumstances, and shaking up the litter into the corners of the box, and selecting and removing certain portions, he grasped the handle of a broom, and swept the pavement as clean as an upper housemaid might be supposed to superintend the sweeping of a breakfast-room of an upper family of great distinction. Then it was that, having spread a light layer of straw over the clean pavement, he proceeded to brush over Sunshine's thighs and hocks, and, discovering a slight stain on the near hind foot, as white as snow from the fetlock to the coronet, proceeded to apply a wet sponge to the temporary blemish with minute care, and smoothed down each particular hair, till the effect bore a close similitude to scraped ivory. Then it was that he proceeded to divide the silky mane into even divisions, and plait them as even and free from straggling hairs as were ever plaited by or for ball-room belle. Then it was that—having completed his task—Puffy Doddles became aware that a somebody, or somebodies, was, or were, about to enter "the box" through that ordinary medium of ingress, the door. Then it was that, upon a sympathising influence of his eyes, acting upon his acute sense of hearing, he discovered the presence of Mr. James Sloper and the head lad of the Great Stable of the North, George Spindles.

Mr. James Sloper never condescended to acknowledge or

even recognise the existence of any retainer in his establishment, excepting. George Spindles, who alone enjoyed, and occasionally revelled in, the exclusive privilege of his confidence.
There were, therefore, no friendly salutations of the morn between Puffy Doddles and his employer upon the advent of the
latter ; but Robert Top's best lad acknowledged the presence
of his superior by raising a thumb and finger, and giving a sudden jerk at a lock of hair which fell conveniently, and as if for
the purpose, over his forehead.

Mr. James Sloper, after making a survey of Sunshine by
"throwing an eye over him," proceeded to his near side, and,
placing a hand over the regions of the heart, appeared, from the
movement of his lips, to be counting its pulsations. He then
moved a step forwards, and, looking at Sunshine's large, full,
lustrous eyes, drew back the lids, and minutely examined the
inner and sensitive parts. Being satisfied, it may be inferred
from the absence of all demonstration to the contrary, of the
general and particular condition of the son of Glitter and Comet,
Mr. James Sloper turned slowly upon his heel, and took his
departure, with a fixed, reflective look bent upon the ground.

The head lad of the Great Stable of the North, during these
operations, employed the moments as they flew by watching
them with a sharp, restless rolling of the eyes, indicative of a
large amount of personal interest. Now, as the end of the skirt
of Mr. James Sloper's long brown coat was about to vanish
through the door of Sunshine's "box," his head, or his hat, or
both, clearly signalised that somebody was to follow. That
" somebody " was George Spindles.

Short was the conference held between Mr. James Sloper
and his head lad. Little, indeed, was said, within a few feet of
the threshold of the door of Sunshine's "box ;" but the few
words, muttered in bated breath, were like those spoken by Fate,
and contained in full the "something up" of Puffy Doddles'
dream.

Newmarket's ghosts and spectres, and things of the night

through which the moon's rays shine unimpeded, vanished as
" the dusky night rolled down the sky and ushered in the morn."
Instead of shades and shadows, phantoms, sprites, hobgoblins,
elf, fay, and fairy having possession of the heath, solid inhabitants of the earth brushed the glittering dewdrops from the
green sward, and flushed the lark to shake her wing in the
early morning sun. Newmarket was awake betimes; but not
too soon for the clearing up of certain mysteries in which Newmarket felt itself deeply interested. Before that frequently-
quoted bird, the early one of the feathered family, had completed
his breakfast, Newmarket arrived at the positive conclusion that
one of the two horses from the Great Stable of the North would
pull off the Two Thousand Guineas. Upon the early one of the
feathered family preening his plumage and polishing his beak
upon a convenient twig, by way of announcement that he had
finished his matin meal, Newmarket had satisfied its doubts and
quieted its fears concerning WHICH of the two horses from the
Great Stable of the North had been selected to pull off the Two
Thousand Guineas. "Sunshine, by Glitter, dam Comet, by
Falling Star, went like a bird. He could give Catch-me-who-
can 7lb. and a beating. Pulled double, and he'd win as he liked,
with plenty to spare, and a little over. Bar accident, and the
race was over. Nothing remained but shouting."

Before the early bird had quite digested his breakfast, it
was announced, on unquestionable authority, that Sunshine was
SCRATCHED.

CHAPTER VII.

"NEWMARKET" was astonished. "The Ring" felt itself
bound to confess "to have been fairly taken by surprise."
"The public" was plunged, in a figurative sense, up to the
very eyelids in "the hole." Puffy Doddles sat upon his accus-
tomed seat, the bottom of a stable-pail, and wiped away not

only one tear, but many. The representatives of the Press gave different versions of "the unexpected result," and expatiated upon "the proverbial uncertainty of the turf." Reports were circulated through that marvellously gifted and eloquent agent, " Rumour," that, " owing to a change of water, change of stable, change of weather, or change of something (not clearly defined), Sunshine coughed, and had to be ' scratched ' at the last moment, and when about to be stripped for the post." The Great Stable of the North, however, was not doomed to disappointment. Failing with the best tried two-year-old out, Catch-me-who-can came to the rescue, and, jumping off with a strong lead, cut the field down in a common canter, winning hard held by ten clear lengths.

Such was the unexpected result for the Two Thousand Guineas in Sunshine's year, whatever might have been the accounts of the finish either before or subsequently.

A few days afterwards, under the head of "Tattersall's," might have been seen a record of the promotion of Catch-me-who-can to the proud place of first favourite for the Derby, at five to three, *taken freely*, while the son of Glitter and Comet receded to fifty to one, *offered*. The former, it is almost unnecessary to add, met with the support of a host of sanguine friends, desirous of evincing their confidence in his merits, while the latter experienced that chilling and even frigid return for coughing that occasionally is termed "getting the cold shoulder." In short, if the " Representatives of the Press " were faithful to their trust, Sunshine's chance of the Derby might be looked upon as gone. Different opinions, however, will both be conceived and expressed upon most subjects, whether social, political, theological, turfical, or otherwise ; and it might have been remarked by an unusually acute observer, that friendless as Sunshine appeared to be, he was not, at least, without that rare, choice, and valuable prop, ' "a friend in need."

The antecedents of Bill Smoothy were, fortunately for the

present position which he held in society, not generally known, and for the sake of public morals, perhaps, it is better that they should remained confined to a limited sphere of knowledge. The ambition of Bill Smoothy, from his boyhood upwards, was to be an associate of the sporting world. Keeping this object steadily in view, and practising a large amount of self-denial in travelling on foot, and frequently with an exhausted exchequer, long and weary journeys from one race meeting to another, and obtaining in the earlier part of his career a far more precarious living than the London sparrows, which are supposed to pick up anything in the shape of crumbs, Bill Smoothy rose, by degrees, to the dignity of a little bookmaker, and, at length, found himself a great commissioner of the highest order, being attached to the Great Stable of the North to make investments for that renowned institution. Like the majority of "sporting characters," Bill Smoothy was peculiar in his personal appearance. Having, possibly, an aversion to the full coat collar of other days, his tailor, acting under instructions, left scarcely a fragment of this part of his outer garment. By a single plain gilt button it was invariably fastened across his breast, and two similar buttons, placed widely apart behind, gave the effect of Bill Smoothy possessing the longest waist of any mortal yet seen, failing to reach the perpendicular of 5 feet 7 inches. With the ordinary tendency of great length of vest in the *attachés* of all stables, Bill Smoothy's waistcoat reached within a few inches of his knee-caps, and his trousers looked much too tight to be pleasant, being buttoned closely round the ankles with no less than three buttons, and giving to view as large a pair of feet, perhaps, and as unsightly a pair of boots, as the eyes of a curious spectator in such objects could possibly desire to rest upon. In the absence of what is generally known as a forehead, Bill Smoothy's round, narrow-brimmed hat was pressed down upon his eyebrows, and his eyes, as black as those of a rat, glistened brightly beneath it. Pale, pimply, and closely shaved were the cheeks, chin, and throat of Bill

Smoothy, and his nose had that hooked or aquiline form which may frequently be seen in the prominent features of the denizens of the Minories. No shadow of a tradition, however, exists for the faintest reasonable conjecture to be formed respecting the birth, parentage, or education of Bill Smoothy. There he stood in the prime of manhood, with a remarkably showy blue and white cravat, tied with scrupulous neatness round his neck, in the subscription-room at Tattersall's occasionally yclept "The Corner," easy in manner, easy in circumstances, and engaged in his usual avocation of adapting the means to the end of easing anybody of any amount of the circulating medium which his superior sagacity might enable him to secure.

"He's as good as a dead 'un, I suppose," remarked Bill Smoothy to an aristocratic member of the Ring, engaged, at this particular moment of the recording of man's doings and misdoings, in making a close examination of the pages of a small pocket-book, and apparently checking the several items contained therein with the fine point of a miniature pencil. "He's as good as a dead 'un, I suppose," repeated the commissioner of the Great Stable of the North.

"Ya-as," drawled out the aristocratic member of the Ring, still keeping his eyes fixed upon the open page of his small volume. "Ya-as," continued he, "there's no doubt o' that;" and then the aristocratic member of the Ring twisted the points of the golden moustache, falling luxuriantly over his upper lip, and smiled as he drew Bill Smoothy's particular attention to an entry in the book with the fine point of his miniature pencil.

"Five thousand to five hundred against Sunshine," perused Bill Smoothy. "Humph! *that* monkey's as good as collared."

"Ya-as," replied the aristocratic member of the Ring, curling his golden moustache round an elaborately-jewelled finger. "I—haugh—flatter myself—haugh—that I may stand that out —haugh!"

"Stand it out!" repeated Bill Smoothy with a sneer. "Catch-me-who-can holds him as safe as if he was boiled."

"Ya-as—haugh," rejoined the aristocratic member of the Ring. "Precisely my idea—haugh."

"You're full, I suppose, against Sunshine?" interrogatively remarked Bill Smoothy, peering out of the corners of his eyes with the expression of a lively ferret upon an approaching but unseen rat.

"Eh!" quickly rejoined the aristocratic member of the Ring, turning back the leaves of his pocket-book with a rapid movement of his fingers. "Eh!—haugh—no; I can go on."

"I've a com, just to suit a book, to back Sunshine for a few ponies," added Bill Smoothy, in a tone and manner which might have led a careless observer to draw the inference of its being a subject of the least importance to the commissioner of the Great Stable of the North whether the ponies were "booked," or turned into cats'-meat on the spot.

"I've—haugh—five thousand to lay—haugh!" observed the aristocratic member of the Ring, after strictly scrutinising the pages of his pocket-book.

"I can take it all at the present price," rejoined Bill Smoothy.

"You are on," smilingly returned the aristocratic member of the Ring. "You are on," repeated he, with an inward and imperfectly concealed chuckle.

The bet was booked. Five thousand to one hundred against Sunshine, by Glitter, dam Comet, by Falling Star. Five thousand to one hundred that he did NOT win the Derby—his next engagement, now on the eve of "coming off."

As Bill Smoothy once remarked—if not more frequently—upon examining the works of a watch which he carried at the terminus of a remarkably thick cable chain of the finest gold, "There are wheels within wheels;" and in the course of this sunny spring afternoon at "Tattersall's" it was remarked by the representatives of the press that, "notwithstanding the

first position of Catch-me-who-can in the betting, occasional
inquiries were made about his stable companion Sunshine, and
in the aggregate a considerable sum was invested upon him at
a long shot."

Mr. James Sloper, be it remarked, was distinguished for
" long shots." By way of a change—in order that there might
be no grounds for a groundless charge of unexceptionable monotony—Mr. James Sloper had, now and then, pressed the hair-
trigger of a certainty at a short range; but as a principle—as
a slender wire which moved his public acts as a public trainer
of a great public stable—Mr. James Sloper preferred giving
rise to public astonishment by hitting the bull's eye at a distance
commonly called " long." His pride was most gratified—to say
nothing of more substantial benefits—in creating a sensation
which the representatives of the press generally described as
"astonishing the Ring." In carrying out this principle, Mr.
James Sloper took particular care to make few, if any, excep-
tions to the rules by which he was governed. As he frequently
observed to his confidential adviser—his inner man—" I never
allow my feelings to interfere with my interests."

Be it, therefore, chronicled that Mr. James Sloper never
permitted his feelings to interfere with his interests.

In the course of this sunny spring afternoon at " Tattersall's "
no " good money " against the best tried two-year-old out
escaped the quiet vigilance of Bill Smoothy and his several
agents; and, singular as it might have seemed, certain books
appeared never quite full against " the crack." But then, of
course, a good bet is never half made until well edged, and the
backers of Catch-me-who-can were merely edging their money,
—merely securing that enviable position figuratively termed
"standing on velvet."

As the shades of evening closed around the pump in
Tattersall's yard on this sunny day, heralding the advent of
summer with incense of flowers and music of birds, and the fox
in the centre was thrown in the form of the Egyptian monster

the Sphynx, upon the white flint stones at its base—hardened when the granite boiled and pure carbon became concentrated in Nature's great laboratory—Bill Smoothy closed his book, and entertained the satisfaction of a man having done his duty.

CHAPTER VIII.

On the eve of the Derby, Puffy Doddles found himself, through the agency of travelling with Sunshine in a van, breathing, for the first time in his life, the remarkably pure atmosphere of the Surrey hills, in the immediaty vicinity of Epsom. A stable, the usual temporary head quarters of the Great Stable of the North, had been prepared for the reception of the colt by Glitter, dam Comet, by Falling Star, and "the lot" trained by Mr. James Sloper for "the great event;" but Puffy Doddles cared nothing about "the lot." The anxious solicitude of Robert Top's best lad was concentrated in ONE of "the lot;" that one, needless be it written, being Sunshine.

Puffy Doddles was full of thought; too full, indeed, to prevent an overflow.

"There you are," said he, stretching out a hand, while the other remained buried in a pocket of his roomy drab knee breeches. "There you are," repeated he, directing the attention of an airy nothing towards Sunshine, who stood in his box, the only palpable auditor of the address, "with a heart as big as a stable bucket, legs like needle-wire, and fit to run for a kingdom or a man's life. You should run for mine," continued Puffy, "if they'd only let me have the mount. Hah!" —and his eyes were fixed upon the ceiling immediately above his head, as he vividly sketched the mental picture—" what a spin that would be!"

Sunshine gave no sign as to the sentiment he entertained upon the stake, or the effort he would make to win it, but stood in a position denoting a dozy, dreamy mood, between sleeping and waking.

"You 're a fizzer," resumed Puffy Doddles, "and in fizzing form"—here Puffy's long-drawn breath hissed between his clenched teeth—"the stable's on, and I am with the stable. There's nothing like being with the stable," continued Sunshine's attendant; "nothing like being in the swim. The public—poor rogues!—stand Catch-me-who-can; but James Sloper, Esquire, I suspect, knows something about the milking game. My eyes, like a kitten's, grow wider as I grow older," concluded Puffy Doddles, with a knowing nod to the Airy Nothing in the corner of the box. "My eyes," repeated he, like a kitten's, "grow wider as I grow older."

As the sun went down, throwing long dark shadows over the Surrey hills and far away, and the mist rose from brook side and valley, and the bee's humming ceased for the drum of the beetle's wing, Puffy Doddles prepared to retire to rest by stretching himself upon a bundle of clean straw, in a corner of Sunshine's box, but with little hope of peaceful slumber. For be it recollected it was "the eve of the Derby," and Robert Top's best lad had nerves.

All that could be accomplished for Sunshine's health, comfort, repose, and happiness, by the prompt attention of his attendant, under the immediate direction of George Spindles, had been observed to the nicest particular. Such was the jealous care that the colt by Glitter, dam Comet, by Falling Star, should not be "got at," that some small live fish had been placed in the water as a preliminary to his drinking it, in order to learn whether subtle poison or injurious drug had been introduced; for it was known that more than one "great bookmaker" had taken great liberties with Sunshine, and had "peppered" him to such an extent that he must have been regarded by these speculators as "safe as if in the liquid state of broth;" and when "great bookmakers" indulge in great liberties of this description, it becomes a matter of considerable care and anxiety on the part of the Slopers, the Spindles, and the Doddles of the stable, to observe due precaution in preventing the exercise of a certain art called "nobbling," by which these "liberties" may be indulged in with impunity. As far, however, as the negative evidence went of entire absence of apparent attempt to "get at" Sunshine, the art had not been put in practice on the present occasion.

In the morning early, and just as the east became tinged with the silver streak of the coming day, Puffy Doddles was up, and stirring. Scarcely, however, had he gained that position known as "upright," when a key, turning harshly in the lock of the stable door, bore testimony to the fact that somebody was coming ; and immediately following the sound, the respective forms, figures, and features of James Sloper and George Spindles were faintly visible in the dark grey and murky light.

"Passed a good night?" interrogatively said Mr. Sloper.

"Very good, sir; I thank you," replied Puffy Doddles, believing, in the innocence of his heart, that the question referred particularly to the manner in which he himself had got through the hours of solitude.

Without any further remark, George Spindles proceeded to rack Sunshine's head up, when Mr. Sloper placed a hand upon the colt's heart; and running it downwards, felt the fore legs and coronets of Sunshine's feet with an action which betokened fear that something might be amiss when least expected.

"You say he passed a good night?" said Mr. Sloper.

Robert Top's best lad now learned that the original question in no way related to himself, and felt that he merited a slight—very slight—castigation that he could have conceived it possible for a moment that it should. Readily, however, was the answer returned in the same words—

"Very good, sir ; I thank you."

The fish exhibiting all the symptoms of strong vitality in the water prepared at hand for Sunshine, he was offered just sufficient to wash his mouth out, introductory to a feed of corn

D

which was thrown into the crib by George Spindles. Then Puffy Doddles commenced the early rub-down, which being completed by the time that Sunshine had finished his corn, a hood, bridle, and saddle were arranged, and, in conformity to the order given, his attendant led him from the box, immediately in front of which stood "the lot" brought from the Great Stable of the North.

No sooner had "the lot" made their appearance on the Downs than numerous representatives of that class known as " Touts" arrived from various points of the compass to watch and learn anything that might be turned to advantage by their employers. Like professors of many arts and sciences, and philosophers both ancient and modern, opinions did not agree among the Touts. One thought that Sunshine had " two big ends and a weak middle." A second that "to win a Derby he'd as soon trust a circus 'oss with eight-stun-ten of bull beef in the saddle." A third curtly remarked, " Don't be too sure o' that. Dead uns win sometimes."

Mr. James Sloper might have heard the last observation ; for as it was made, a close observer would have seen a slight drawing back of the angles of his mouth, as if he felt its force rather pleasurable than otherwise.

At the close of the hour's walk, Sunshine returned to his box, and, being regarded as started only to make the running for Catch-me-who-can, escaped, what may be called, general observation. A few, however, a truly select few, watched every muscle as he moved ; and the " good thing" became better, in the sight of this select few, as it waxed older.

Now it was that the colt by Glitter, dam Comet, by Falling Star, had six go-downs of water—the fish therein being seen to exhibit as lively symptoms of vitality as before ; and then Puffy Doddles stripped to the waist with a smile of perfect confidence, to give him the final dressing previous to—as was supposed— his being started to make the running for his stable companion, Catch-me-who-can. Now it was that the head lad, George

SUNSHINE PREPARING FOR "THE DERBY."

Spindles, exercised his nicest skill in plaiting Sunshine's mane and his shoes being removed by the smith in attendance for this express purpose, the plates were adjusted, and the preparation for the post almost completed. A full feed of corn was thrown into the crib, and as soon as finished the setting-muzzle was buckled on, and then each and all left the colt by Glitter, dam Comet, by Falling Star, to chew the cud, possibly, of reflection.

Little more than three hours previous to that fixed for the race to be numbered with the past, Mr. James Sloper, George Spindles, and Puffy Doddles again entered Sunshine's box. A double handful of corn was presented during the process of a final rubbing down, at the conclusion of which the best two-year-old out stood fit, in his three-year-old form, to add new honours to those already won, or to materially dim their lustre.

CHAPTER IX.

THE race was over.

It might be described as briefly as most races, if the saving of space were a matter of considerable importance. Sunshine took the lead, kept it, and WON HARD HELD.

Men stared at each other aghast. As a matter of course, some said they had been "done," others thought so in moody silence, and a great number felt so without making known their sentiments either in looks or words. Mr. James Sloper had very little to say upon the subject: "The horses were started to run on their merits; and if the public backed the wrong one, *that* was no business of his." Nothing could be more conclusive. For what possible business could it be to Mr. James Sloper whether the public backed the right horse or the wrong horse ?

The commissioner to the Great Stable of the North Bill

Smoothy, might, probably, have given an answer. That saga-
cious individual knew, from experience, the business, combined
with pleasure, which may be done effectually when the public
fall into a little mistake of this kind. As the means to the end
of filling certain pockets, he deemed it, among the many, "one
of the best games out!"

But what were the sentiments of Puffy Doddles upon this
momentous occasion? From the moment the bell began to ring
for saddling, to that when Sunshine's number was hoisted first
on the telegraph as the winner of the Derby, Robert Top's
best lad felt that he was not exactly master of his own sayings
or doings. He knew just sufficient, however, to be aware that
he maintained his perpendicular, and that his heels did not
occupy the ordinary position of his head.

"I think it's all right," said he, in that silent language
when man communes with his inward man, as he led Sunshine,
followed by Catch-me-who-can, in the paddock, just previous to
the signal being made for saddling. "I think it's all right,"
repeated he to himself; "but until the jock's weighed in, and
the clerk o' the scales gives the office of 'all right,' I'll be
blessed if a race is won. A backer of hosses"—and Puffy
Doddles referred particularly to himself—"should think o'
this."

Whether this train of thought, suggestive of self-preserva-
tion to "backers of hosses" would have been continued, or
otherwise, had not the shrill sound of a bell caused a visible
sensation in the crowd around, and in not one of that crowd
more than in Puffy Doddles, it is needless to inquire; but no
sooner was it heard, than Robert Top's best lad cut short the
thread of his meditation, and devoted his energies, both mental
and physical, to action.

"Now, then," said George Spindles, with two large hectic
spots upon his cheeks, and flashing eyes, "look alive."

Nothing, and no one, could look more lively than Puffy
Doddles appeared upon receiving these brief but expressive

instructions. To say that he skipped, would poorly convey the action of his legs; and to add that his arms began a windmill movement in a strong gale, is a feeble description of what they seemed ready to accomplish.

In the twinkling of something as bright as a diamond or dew-drop, Puffy Doddles stripped the light clothing from Sunshine's sleek and shining coat; and as soon as the task could be accomplished through human agency, a saddle was adjusted and securely girthed upon his back, and the colt by Glitter, dam Comet, by Falling Star, stood ready for "the mount."

Scarcely was the preparation complete, when a small man, with sunken eyes and high cheek bones, standing near, and engaged in what would appear to be a discussion of deep interest with Mr. James Sloper, threw off a silver drab overcoat, decorated with buttons as large as oyster-shells, which hitherto had concealed his under garments, and revealed to view a spare, bony figure, dressed in yellow and black.

As if fascinated on the spot, Puffy Doddles stared with blinkless eyelids at the spare, bony figure, dressed in yellow and black, as if he desired to learn by a look of inquiry something about what was covered by these wasp-like colours.

In the professional method of seeking assistance, the figure in the wasp-like colours raised a leg; and, through the "lift-up" of George Spindles, he threw himself lightly, and with the ease of a bird, into the saddle, and Sunshine stood "mounted for the Derby."

It was a great moment in the life of Puffy Doddles to behold *his* horse ready to start for the first time; and that, too, for a great race. His eyes were riveted upon, and he saw nothing else but *his* horse. As he walked by the side of *his* horse from the paddock towards the race course, he heard but one remark in which he took the most finitessimal interest—"That's Sunshine;" the alloy to his pride and pleasure being that *his* horse, as yet, played second fiddle; but—as he said without fear of contradiction, speaking as he did only to his inward man, "Wait a bit."

The time described as "a bit" was of short duration.

The last words spoken by Mr. James Sloper to the spare, bony figure in the wasp-like colours, as he bent forward in his saddle to receive the final instructions, were, "Strangle 'em !"

To his inward man—for Puffy Doddles heard them as distinctly as words that were ever spoken within the reach of his hearing—Robert Top's best lad repeated, "Strangle 'em !"

Then there was a roar, "They 're off."

The bell clanged again.

" Hats off !" was thundered.

" Here they come."

" Sunshine leads."

" Merry wins."

" Sir Joseph wins."

" Sunshine," screamed a single voice, so shrill and clear that it was heard far above the general din, "Sunshine wins !"

This was the fiat shrieked by Puffy Doddles, in anticipation of that given by the judge.

Sunshine had " STRANGLED 'EM !"

CHAPTER X.

THE public now possessed one of those few results, in anticipation, which might be regarded as "a booked certainty" recorded by Nemesis. The forthcoming St. Leger being among Sunshine's engagements, public running proved, beyond the shadow of a doubt in the minds of the most sceptical, that not a horse in the race had a chance with the colt by Glitter, dam Comet, by Falling Star. Fit at the post, and nothing could beat him. Such was the confident opinion expressed by the cosmopolite "everybody"—let it be repeated—that "nothing could beat him."

Sipping his claret one evening in his snuggery, Mr. James Sloper might have been seen, had the opportunity been afforded, to rub the tips of his fingers together with that cat-like movement to which reference has been made on a former occasion.

"A great deal o' money," said he to the Invisible, to whom alone he confided his thoughts when arranging plans for the future. "A great deal o' money," repeated he, "might be made out o' this oss. The public have backed, and will back, nothing else." Here Mr. James Sloper held a glass of claret to the light, and appeared to be scrutinising its colour; but a close observer would have seen that he neither saw the glass nor the wine. "It's a great stake, too," continued he; "and one that I should like to win. Now the question is what shall I do, win or lose? I can't do both," and Mr. James Sloper's teeth came together with a snap, expressive of great discontent that he could not do both. "With the money lumped on as it is, they'd give the price of a county to have him pulled," resumed he; "and to back him at the present odds it's like giving one pound one for a sovereign. It's buying money too dear."

Mr. James Sloper tossed off the glass of claret; but it might have been vinegar and water as far as any appreciable effect was produced.

Some seconds elapsed before he resumed his thinking aloud; and the interval was employed in gently chafing the ends of his fingers, as if the action not only promoted circulation, but materially assisted in continuing the train of thought.

"Bar accident," he resumed, still addressing the Invisible and Airy Nothing in the remote corner of the apartment. "Bar accident," repeated he, "and" — the words dropped slowly, one by one from his lips like peas—"I'll win it; but" — and here he seemed to have hit upon something unusually felicitous—"I must be on at a longer figger than five to two. What shall he have? A bad night won't do. That would be found out too soon. A tight bandage?" Mr. James Sloper shook his head.

Shaking the head of Mr. James Sloper might possibly possess a corresponding effect to that of shaking a pepper-castor; for what was desired seemed to be produced at once through the agency of the action.

"I have it," said he, with a chuckle; and his laugh was so subdued, that it must have been a quick ear to have caught the faintest effect of it, placed, as it might have been, close to the keyhole of the door. "I have it," repeated he; "and some of 'em shall get a hot un this time."

A few more hours had passed since Mr. James Sloper formed the scheme of preparing a warm presentation for the undefined noun of multitude, when he might have been seen entering a box, on the door of which was now nailed a plate encircled with the words, in a garter, "Sunshine, winner of the Derby, 18—."

As usual, Puffy Doddles was at the post of duty at that precise moment of the world's history when he was expected to be.

As usual, Robert Top's best lad, upon the advent of his master, made his best bow; and if not combined with the ease and elegance of that of a courtier, was intended, at least, to be quite as respectful towards a superior.

Mr. James Sloper coughed in a manner which denoted that, after clearing his voice, he was about to speak.

Puffy Doddles, ever obedient, from the moment he learned his first lesson, upon entering a training stable, "to keep his hands down, and hold his tongue," felt that his superior was about to confer upon him the honour of addressing him, and made known his readiness to listen by a deferential pull at the piece of straight hair sprouting in the centre of his forehead in the form of a duck's tail.

Mr. James Sloper coughed a second time.

Robert Top's best lad again signified his prepared condition to be a willing listener then and there, by a pull, which may be described as little short of " detonating," at the straight piece of hair sprouting in the centre of his forehead in the form of a duck's tail.

" You know what ' mum' means, don't ye ? " interrogated his employer, with a sullen, scowling look, which slowly measured Puffy Doddles from heel to head.

" To hold my tongue, sir," blandly replied Robert Top's best lad, with a fidgetty shuffle of his feet.

" Ex-actly so," rejoined Mr. James Sloper, staring Puffy Doddles so unpleasantly in the face, that it became flushed with heat, and bore the appearance of having been roasted, and rather " over done " in an incredibly short space of time. " Ex-actly so," repeated he. " That's it. To hold your tongue. Mind and recollect that ' mum ' means to hold your tongue."

Puffy Doddles thought—but adopted the wise precaution of giving no expression to the thought—that as he had conveyed a prompt and correct definition of ' mum,' the necessity was small, if not altogether limited beyond the sense of comprehension, for Mr. James Sloper to echo the sentiment in the very same words used by himself.

" Now, finding you know what ' mum ' means," resumed Mr. James Sloper, " just give your attention to what I am going to say."

Puffy Doddles looked the personification of attention.

" You'll give him "—Mr. James Sloper jerked his head towards Sunshine—" a good, rousing gallop this morning."

Robert Top's best lad felt a warm, expanding glow of pleasure spread through his system at the exhilarating diversion in store.

" As you come to Chalk Hill at a canter, mend the pace, and "—here Mr. James Sloper raised a forefinger, as if to draw particular attention to what he was about to add—" as you come to the turn of the lands, hold him well together, and, with your heels in his ribs, send him straight across the arable."

Puffy Doddles gave a sob, as if his breath had been suddenly taken away.

"Sit back in your saddle, as if sawing his head off," continued Mr. James Sloper; "but keep your heels in his ribs, and don't pull him."

Robert Top's best lad began to speculate, under these circumstances, where he should arrive at last.

"When across the arable, and it will fly as you go, I know," said Mr. James Sloper, seeing, in his mind's eye, the clouds of dust which must be left in Sunshine's track, "keep on over the Downs; and upon reaching the top of One Tree Hill, go gingerly down the slope, and then stop him as soon as ye can."

The instructions appeared to be complete; but Puffy Doddles still remained in an attitude of profound attention.

"You'll not let him *really* get away with you?" said Mr. James Sloper, in the form of a question.

"He'll not try, sir," briefly replied Robert Top's best lad, with his eyes fixed upon the floor of the box.

"I know that you can do anything with the 'oss," added Sunshine's trainer. "Mind, and do this; and do it well."

Puffy Doddles made a practical reference to the duck's tail, and sighed deeply.

———

CHAPTER XI.

GREAT was the commotion in the sporting world. Messages were sent flying along "the wires" to the effect that "Sunshine had run away with the lad at exercise, and pulled up dead lame." Tempting baits were offered by the bookmakers on the spot. Instead of five to two being the quoted market price, six, seven, and even eight to one went begging. Such, at least, was the "official report" of the odds offered against Sunshine upon the intelligence being received of his having "run away with the lad at exercise."

An "official report," however, of a later date, announced that "towards the afternoon the strong current which had set in against the favourite earlier in the day met with a decided check, and before the close of the afternoon anything over four to one was taken freely." The inhabitants of the earth had scarcely become either older or humbler, when a third "official report" was circulated that "the friends of Sunshine rallied in such force that so far from any symptoms existing of the likelihood of his being 'knocked out,' layers became so shy that three to one could hardly be obtained, and many books were closed against him." Then followed a fourth "official report :"— "We learn that the rumour of Sunshine having overpowered his lad while at exercise was quite in accordance with the fact; but that his having pulled up dead lame may be construed as an unequivocal exaggeration of the mischief. In order to learn the worst that might have happened under such circumstances, his trainer, Mr. James Sloper, immediately called in the services of the eminent veterinary surgeon, Professor Doeland, and that gentleman, after a careful examination, pronounced a most decided opinion that the colt had received no injury whatever. The reinstatement of Sunshine as first favourite in the betting must prove highly satisfactory to his influential party, and the public in general, who have supported him throughout in a manner which proves the immense confidence entertained in his capacity to pull off the double event."

Mr. James Sloper perused the details of the fourth "official report" with a relish approaching the indescribable. He rubbed the ends of his fingers together, and his inward chuckle might have been accepted for the pur-r-r of a cat without any great stretch upon the imagination. Never did the claret taste better, never did it look more brilliant, as Mr. James Sloper held it to the light previous to bringing it in contact with his lips for the consummation of enjoyment.

"It was as good a movement as was ever made to get on at a better figger," said Mr. James Sloper to the transparent and airy nothing, the sole companion of these musings aloud. "It was as good a movement as was ever made," repeated he with a smack of his lips which sounded not unlike the crack of a whip, "to get on at a better figger. That lad, I saw, didn't like the job of making a sham run away," continued Mr. James Sloper, "and I shan't trust him with any more moves of a similar kind. He's a leetle too honest, I see; a leetle too honest, I see. It's a rare quality though," said he, with a smile closely linked to a sneer. "One doesn't often meet with too much honesty. There'd be more fools than rogues in the world if honesty was plentiful, and I'll be blest if that's the case in these times!"

At this juncture a slight announcement was made of somebody being outside the door of Mr. James Sloper's snuggery, and signifying, through the agency of a subdued tap, tap, tap, evidently with knuckles, that he or she—as the case might be—required permission to place himself, or herself—in accordance with circumstances over which he or she had no control—inside the door of Mr. James Sloper's snuggery.

"Come in," shouted Sunshine's trainer.

The spare and bony figure, whilom dressed in the wasp-like colours, entered an appearance.

"Oh! it's you, Johnny, is it?" exclaimed Mr. James Sloper. "Glad you're come. Sit down, and make yourself comfortable."

With this friendly invitation, Mr. James Sloper pushed the bottle of claret across the table, and urged "Johnny" to fill a glass with the utmost expedition, after occupying a part of a chair opposite his host; for such were the abridged and narrow dimensions of that spare and bony figure, that to do more than occupy part of a chair was simply impossible.

"Glad you're come," reiterated Mr. James Sloper.

"Thank'e, sir. Glad I am," responded Johnny; but as far as any outward and visible sign was concerned, the happiness of neither seemed greatly augmented.

"Anything up?" briefly inquired Sunshine's trainer.

"Nothing partickler, sir," replied Johnny, clearly proving at this moment that he had no idea of sipping claret.

"Anything up that's *not* particular?" rejoined his entertainer.

"Nothing that *I* know of," returned the spare and bony figure.

"Anything up that anybody else knows of?" pertinaciously inquired Mr. James Sloper.

"Can't say," responded Johnny; "but shouldn't be struck of a heap if there is."

It is worthy of record, perhaps, that these words were spoken in a peculiarly severe and caustic tone, as if the speaker meant much more than he said.

"You've come to learn about this last dodge," added Mr. James Sloper; "and what has been done, or is to be done for you."

Johnny appeared to consider it quite unnecessary to offer any remark upon the suggested object of his visit, as no more correct reading of his inmost thoughts could have been presented even by himself.

"In other words," resumed Sunshine's trainer, "you want to know what's meant."

The spare and bony figure nodded mechanically.

"Then we understand each other," continued Mr. James Sloper, "without much talking on both sides."

Johnny quite coincided in this opinion, but left Mr. James Sloper to draw whatever inference he thought proper or expedient.

"*I* pulled the strings," said Sunshine's trainer, speaking metaphorically.

Johnny never entertained the smallest doubt as to the particular fingers manipulating the strings.

"You're on now——"

The spare and bony figure leaned forward in his chair.

"A monkey to nothing," concluded Mr. James Sloper.

" Then——"

" Yes," interrupted his entertainer, "the stable money's on, and he runs to win."

" Glad of it," replied Johnny ; " I began to think the milking can was set to work."

" A good many others began to think so too," rejoined Mr. James Sloper, taking from a breast-pocket in his coat a volume which possessed the unmistakeable appearance of a betting book, and turning over its pages with a damped thumb, repeated in a slow, deliberate manner, " A good many others began to think so too."

" So help me potaters!" exclaimed Johnny, with great exultation expressed both in tone and manner ; "it was a well-planned, well-worked dodge. It almost dropped me in the hole, it did ; so help me potaters!"

' " You don't mean that ?" ejaculated Mr. James Sloper, shutting his volume with a sudden snap.

" I do," returned Johnny. " I do, so help me potaters!"

" Ha, ha, ha!" roared Sunshine's trainer. " Ha, ha, ha! Tell us all about it. Ha, ha, ha!"

" Well," added Johnny, " it came off in this way. I saw Sweety at the corner——"

" Sweety!" echoed Mr. James Sloper, raising his eyebrows, and looking as if an explosion of mirth was about to follow. " You don't mean to tell me that thief——"

" I do," said Johnny ; " I do, so help me potaters!"

" Ha, ha, ha!" again roared Sunshine's trainer. " Ha, ha, ha! To think that we got at that thief at last!"

" I saw Sweety at the corner," resumed Johnny, " and he told me that he knew every guinea laid against our hoss was as good as won."

" Did he really ?" returned Mr. James Sloper, rolling back in his chair, and having all the appearance of being almost convulsed with joy.

" Knowing what a deep and artful card Sweety is," continued Johnny, "I thought I couldn't do better than lay against him, and had a good mind to send out a commission to pepper him like blue blazes."

"But you didn't?" said Mr. James Sloper, checking his laugh.

"As luck would have, I didn't," responded Johnny; "but"—and here he looked as serious as if the risk incurred was much too hazardous to be pleasant—"I was as near as a toucher, so help me potaters!"

"No matter," cried Sunshine's trainer; "on the post by a short head does for me as well as a clear length, or twenty lengths, for that matter. Fill your glass, Johnny. I'll order a fresh bottle."

CHAPTER XII.

DONCASTER was in her holiday gear. Doncaster had donned her best bib and tucker. The mayor and corporation of Doncaster—especially the mayor—felt what the weight and care of office really were during the great Doncaster meeting, and did not hesitate to declare deep sympathy with the Czar of all the Russias, to say nothing of the manifold duties of the Secretary of State for the Home Department. The High Street, as was its wont, on the great day of the great meeting, looked proud of itself, and totally indifferent to the vanity displayed in the bye-streets, adjacent to, leading from, and bounded by the main artery of the corporate town of Doncaster. Flags of many colours, tints, and hues flaunted in the breeze, and merry peals of bells sent forth their silvery music, announcing as plainly as metal tongues could speak that it was the "Leger Day." If all Yorkshire were not present, a large portion of that northern community had resolved to be witnesses of the anticipated triumph of the "Great Stable of the North," and recreant and renegade would he have been deemed to his faith and county who, Yorkshire bred, had expressed even a doubt that Sunshine would fail to add the St. Leger prize to his Derby victory.

The colt was well, and fit to run for the ransom of a kingdom. Such was the "official report" of Sunshine's condition on the eventful morning of the race. "The talent" ventured to declare that "nothing could beat him." The favourite had the call of the field at five to four, and "the talent," to a man, declared that "nothing could beat him."

It is not known whether Puffy Doddles either considered himself, or was considered by others, as a member of "the talent;" but whether so or otherwise, he entertained a corresponding balance of confidence in *his* horse with this distinguished body, and felt inwardly, as he expressed outwardly, that "nothing could beat him." All that could be done to bring the colt by Glitter, dam Comet, by Falling Star, to the post in as fine condition as it was possible for unintermitting care, attention, and watchfulness to accomplish, had been observed with the utmost strictness; and as he walked in his strength and beauty, with head erect, and proud and dainty tread, ready for saddling, Robert Top's best lad felt, as he led him as gently as a lamb held by silken thread, that if possessed of the hidden treasure in the vaults of the Bank of England, he would trust him with the last sovereign contained therein. For be it understood that Puffy Doddles knew that he was "meant."

The tongue of the bell for saddling had scarcely given forth its noisy note for preparation, when George Spindles proceeded to strip Sunshine of his clothing; and as his light, muscular frame became exposed to view, and his glossy coat shone like burnished copper in the sun, a murmur of admiration broke from the lips of those around, and the most critical had not a fault to find.

Just at this moment, however, and as George Spindles was passing the rubber over his glistening skin, which varied in the light like shot-silk, Sunshine was seen to lash out his near

SUNSHINE SHOWING TEMPER.

hind leg in a manner which betokened mischief to all or any within reach.

"Come, I say," observed Puffy Doddles, in a tone of reproach, and looking at *his* horse in the face with impromptu severity, "what are you about, I should like to know?"

George Spindles glanced at the horse from ear to heel, and stood for a moment with the rubber unemployed.

Sunshine made a playful snap at Robert Top's best lad's left shoulder, as much as to say, "Take care, or I'll eat *you*, bones and buttons!"

"So there! Gently, my la-ad!" exclaimed George Spindles, again applying the rubber to Sunshine's sleek sides. Scarcely, however, had he touched him, when the horse flung out both heels, and, with his head between his knees, continued a succession of kicks which, in rapidity of movement, combined with strength, were never excelled, and rarely equalled.

George Spindles did not turn pale, but his complexion bore on the instant the tint of a green bronze.

"What's the matter?" gasped Mr. James Sloper, arriving with the spare and bony figure ready for "the mount."

"He's showing temper," whispered George Spindles, "and hang me if I know what to think!"

"Stand aside!" passionately ejaculated Mr. James Sloper, snatching the saddle from the jockey's arms, and approaching Sunshine with the design of placing it upon his back. Vain, however, was the attempt; for no sooner did he raise the saddle than Sunshine plunged away kicking, and dragging Puffy Doddles with him, in a manner likely to produce dislocation in more joints than one.

It was an awful moment for Messrs. Sloper, Spindles, and Johnny, to say nothing of the feelings of "the party" standing around.

"Oh!" groaned one of "the party," "we shan't get even a start for any money."

"We're dropped into a pretty hole!" whined a second.

E

"I could cut his throat!" added a third, savagely. "It's the stock, all over. The most uncertain brutes that ever looked through bridles: fly when they like, and stand still when they don't!"

Mr. James Sloper felt dizzy, and the ground immediately under his feet began to waltz. A ready thought, however, seemed to take possession of his brain as to what was expedient under the pressing emergency of the case.

"Here," said he, thrusting the saddle into the hands of Puffy Doddles, and relieving him of the reins; "see what you can do."

The moment that Robert Top's best lad went to Sunshine's near side he became as quiet and tractable as a perfectly broken lady's palfrey. Not the smallest objection was evinced to have the saddle placed and girthed upon his back by Puffy Doddles, who completed the task in a manner which both won and commanded the admiration of all beholders.

Messrs. Sloper, Spindles, and Johnny, together with "the party," breathed again.

It was, however, a breath of momentary duration; for no sooner did the spare and bony figure in the wasp-like colours step forward for the "lift up," than Sunshine wheeled round, as if on a pivot, and sent out his heels in a direct line with the elevation of Johnny's head. So close did those flying, iron-shod heels come to Johnny's head that he felt the sudden puff of wind from them in his face. A short inch closer, and the spare and bony figure in the wasp-like colours would have been

"A thing
O'er which the raven flaps her funeral wing."

Again and again did Johnny essay his most skilful attempts to approach Sunshine's near side, but with no better success. The horse would not allow him to come nearer than just about the reach of his heels, when, wheeling round, he threw them out with a vengeance which showed the depth of his antipathy to his intended rider.

"It's no use," said Mr. James Sloper, in a voice husky with anxiety. "It's no use," repeated he. "We have but one chance;" and, clutching Puffy Doddles by an arm, he dragged him away, roughly, through the crowd.

CHAPTER XIII.

PUFFY DODDLES was quite sensible of being dragged roughly through the crowd. His toe₋ trodden upon; his ribs punched by angular elbows; his features rubbed against by knobby substances; the bow of his cravat turned directly under his left ear; his cap thrust most unbecomingly over his eyes, and his jacket pulled from his shoulders to pinion him by the elbows in a position of extreme helplessness, bore conclusive evidence of his having been dragged roughly through the crowd. Mr. James Sloper vouchsafed no syllable of explanation for the proceeding; but, upon arriving at the weighing-room, Robert Top's best lad received instructions "to strip," and scarcely was this mandate responded to when he found himself, with harlequin dispatch, equipped in boots and breeches—a trifle too large—and the wasp-like colours, yellow and black.

"Quick!" shouted Mr. James Sloper, giving Puffy Doddles a push which sent him staggering back, and landing him deftly —to use a piscatorial phrase—in the scale behind.

A saddle having been placed in Puffy Doddles' lap, one or two weights shifted, some dead weight, in the shape of shotted cloths, added to the specific gravity of Robert Top's best lad, and that important functionary, "the Clerk of the Scales," announced it was "all right."

"Weighed for the Leger," somebody or something seemed to whisper to Puffy Doddles; but, notwithstanding what he saw, and felt, and knew was passing immediately around, he could not divest himself of the lurking fear of its being a dream, and very ideal nothing of the brain.

"Come, look alive !" said Mr. James Sloper, sharply, as he again seized Puffy Doddles by the arm, and conducted him, in an excited manner, bordering on apparent delirium, from the weighing-room.

"Listen," said he, as they again threaded their way through the crowd.

Puffy Doddles was ready to listen, with an intensity of interest far removed and beyond the ordinary powers of language to describe.

" He'll let you ride him, and nobody else to-day."

The heart of Puffy Doddles knocked against his bosom with ill-concealed pride as these words were spoken, in a tone of bitter disappointment, by his employer.

"He *may* run kindly for you," continued Mr. James Sloper ; "and if so, all you've got to do is to sit still. D'ye understand ? "

Puffy Doddles thought he knew, as well as any one living, what sitting still was, and said so without the smallest reservation.

" Catch-me-who-can," resumed Mr. James Sloper, "will make the running for ye, and he'll cut it out as strong as he can make it. As soon as his bolt's shot, come to the front ; but recollect, not before."

Indelible was the impression in Puffy Doddles' memory that he must not come to the front previous to the shooting of the particular bolt referred to.

"Then," concluded Mr. James Sloper, bringing his lips close to the nearest ear belonging to Robert Top's best lad, " break their hearts."

Such were the last words of the first order given to Puffy Doddles for riding his maiden race—" Break their hearts."

Just before the start—as the "official report" subsequently declared—"there was quite a commotion in the ring. It becoming known that Sunshine had turned restive, and refused to be even saddled, excepting by the stable lad having the charge of him, and that such was the violent temper exhibited by the colt that the jockey engaged to ride him had to be supplanted by this boy, the odds from being five to four on the favourite, taken freely, suddenly veered to two to one on the field."

An eye-witness remarked that "Sunshine's backers looked blue as indigo when the stable lad was 'put up,' instead of one of the most accomplished riders of the day."

Puffy Doddles, with features bearing the hue and tint of an unhealthy turnip, sat in the saddle, nevertheless, with the grace and ease that might have been expected from Robert Top's best lad, and as he stooped forward to pat and caress the arched neck of *his* horse, more than one practised eye and good judge proclaimed that "the boy could ride."

With hands down, and standing in his stirrups, so that the horse swept beneath him in long, lurching strides, without moving a bone, thew, or sinew of his frame, Puffy Doddles took the preliminary canter, and pulled up amidst a buzz of admiration.

"The boy could ride, and the horse went like a bird," was the opinion of more than one practised eye and good judge.

"Who put you on a race-'oss?" inquired one of the "old school" of jockeys, "taking stock" of Sunshine and Robert Top's best lad, with a sneer of contempt.

"I'll let you know at the finish," was the spirited and prompt reply of Puffy Doddles.

"Let me know at the finish!" repeated he of the "old school," looking, at that moment, as if a most offensive smell had suddenly come "between the wind and his nobility." "Might as well," continued he, "have put up so many stone o' cow beef."

Puffy Doddles felt what may be truly called savage at this rejoinder; but the responsibility of his position quickly dissipated the sentiment, and, as he turned *his* horse to go to the post, he resolved that no temptation should prevail upon his doing otherwise than riding strictly to the orders he had received.

"I wonder if I shall ever have a mount for a Great St. Leger ?"

Who asked that question, just as Robert Top's best lad was going to join the field of horses at the post ?

Even at that important moment Puffy Doddles glanced both right and left to solve the mystery ; but perceiving no one near who could have made such an inquiry, came to the correct conclusion that he was merely repeating a question which he had propounded to himself at an earlier period of his biography.

Robert Top's best lad now cast all thoughts aside but one—to ride to orders, and do his best.

The start was delayed for some time in consequence of several breaking in anticipation of the signal ; but it was remarked that Sunshine displayed no single symptom of fractiousness. The colt by Glitter, dam Comet, by Falling Star, appeared to have taken upon himself, without the smallest preparation, the nature of a turtle dove, in so far as quietness was concerned. "Go!" the flag dropped; and "They're off!" were the several notifications that the race had begun.

With the character of a good beginner, Catch-me-who-can rushed to the front, and cut out the work at a pace which the "official report" announced as "terrific." Away he streaked, like a meteor, cutting down the field, and producing those "tailing" effects which quickly extinguished the fervent hopes of many a sanguine supporter of an "off chance."

"They'll never catch him," cried a voice, the proprietor of which was minutely scanning every inch of the race through a powerful glass.

"Who leads ?" inquired a by-stander, not so well prepared for bringing a wide range within closer limits of vision.

"Catch-me-who-can," rejoined he with the glass. "What against Catch-me-who-can ?"

"Five to one," was the ready answer, given by a certain commissioner standing close to the elbow of the questioner, and bearing the plebeian name of Bill Smoothy. "Five to one, sir," repeated he, with a bland smile, opening a small volume, and gently poising, between a thumb and finger, a finely-pointed pencil.

"Done for a hundred!" returned the supporter of Catch-me-who-can. "I'll take," continued he, "five hundred to a hundred that Catch-me-who-can wins."

With additional blandness in the smile, Bill Smoothy proceeded to record the bet, and, as he did so, he muttered, in a tone only audible to himself, "Catch-'em-alive."

With a swing round the corner into the straight ground a lot of horses was seen to come; the gay, bright, and varied colours of the riders fluttering in the breeze, and looking, in the distance, like so many full-blown tulips.

"Who leads now?" shouted a voice.

"Catch-me-who-can," was the reply; "and Catch-me-who-can wins."

A certain commissioner standing near smiled still more blandly.

Just at this moment, however, it was loudly announced by a hundred voices that "Catch-me-who-can was beaten."

Now it was that the leader's bolt having been shot, Puffy Doddles eased the strong pull upon Sunshine's jaws, and, like an arrow, the gallant horse rushed to the front; and, upon reaching the distance-post, the cry "Sunshine wins!" rent the air. Now it was that Robert Top's best lad sat in his saddle as still as an Egyptian mummy might have been supposed to have done. Hands down and motionless, Puffy Doddles glanced at the struggling competitors by his side, among whom was the jockey of "the old school," and quitting them—as the "official report" declared—"with ridiculous ease, went in a winner by six clear lengths."

Sunshine had BROKEN THEIR HEARTS.

CHAPTER XIV.

LAVISH was the praise bestowed upon Puffy Doddles for the consummate skill and judgment displayed by him in riding the winner of the Great St. Leger. A finer bit of jockeyship was never seen, if that which everybody said might be construed as being correct ; and Mr. James Sloper not only slapped Robert Top's best lad between the shoulders, upon returning to scale, accompanying the action of approval with a familiar "Well done !" but added, "Before you're much older, you'll find yourself a good deal richer."

And Mr. James Sloper kept his implied promise to increase the worldly possessions of Puffy Doddles with the utmost strictness. Before the close of another day his employer announced that he held to the credit of Robert Top's best lad a comfortable nest egg, in the shape of two hundred and fifty pounds, to be delivered in part, or otherwise, whenever and wherever he thought fit or expedient.

The communication caused Puffy Doddles to gasp not unlike a newly landed and stranded fish. Being dumb-founded, it was impossible for him to return thanks in words, however brief and simple ; and adopting, as it seemed to him, the only alternative, he continued to pull in silence the piece of hair sprouting luxuriantly, as of yore, upon his forehead, with a degree of vengeance which threatened to tear it up by the roots.

" That'll do," remarked Mr. James Sloper, considerately. "Don't pull your head off. I shall want the use of your head again some day."

Puffy Doddles felt greatly flattered to find that his head was now at a premium.

Together, and alone, Robert Top's best lad stood gazing at *his* horse with a fondness of expression which the language of good poetry might possibly describe, but which ordinary prose must certainly fail to pourtray.

"The winner of the double event!" soliloquised he, standing with arms folded across his breast. "The *un*beaten one in every engagement they have pulled ye out for! It wouldn't be right, I suppose," continued he, "to go down on my knees and wusshup ye; but if there ever was a real, living idol, in the shape of a race-'oss, you're mine!"

Sunshine lifted a hind foot just an inch or two from the litter, and threw back both ears, as much as to say, "None o'· your gammon!"

"You are," resumed Puffy Doddles, "my own real, living idol; and well you may be. Here was I only yesterday mornin' as ever was, a poor, and pretty nigh friendless, stable lad. Now what's the consequence? Look at me at this present time. Talked about, written about, praised right and left, patted on the back like a dorg that's won the fight, stared at and admired as though I was a Prince of the Blood Royal, coaxed, and sugary-treacled, and paid more for three minutes and fifteen seconds' work than a full-blown man could earn by hard work in seven years. And who have I got to thank?"

The colt by Glitter, dam Comet, by Falling Star, made a playful snap with his teeth, as much as to say, "If you mean me, take care, or I'll eat ye."

"If I was doomed to be swallered," continued Robert Top's best lad, "you should do it before any 'oss or halligator that was ever foaled; but I hope that's not my latter end just at present. I want to live and ride ye to the front, and over and over again to 'break their hearts.' That's what *I* want to do;" and Puffy Doddles touched the middle button of his light holland stable jacket, so that no error might exist in reference to the personal desire.

Sunshine gave a suppressed and rather uneuphonious squeak, clearly intimating that to break more hearts would prove a source of considerable enjoyment to him.

"And then when your last race was run"—here Puffy Doddles might have been seen to screw the bent knuckles of his two forefingers into the corners of his eyes, and the breast of his light holland stable-jacket to heave somewhat convulsively—"and then when your last race was run," repeated he, in a voice anything but steady, " I should like to be in a situation to refuse all offers to ride again."

Sunshine evidently felt the compliment paid, with such sincerity, to his merits and virtues, and stretched himself out in a proud position to listen attentively to the sequel.

" I should never wish to ride another," resumed Robert Top's best lad, shaking his head. "Fifty-two pounds a year, a cottage near a wood, a Missis Puffy just to look after my linen, and make my gruel when a little off, is all I shall want, old feller, when your last race is run."

Sunshine again squeaked an unmusical squeak, signifying conclusively that " he wished he might get the annuity, domain, and a better half, precisely in accordance with the proclaimed details, and strictly for the purposes declared."

"In that case," said Puffy Doddles, " I should feel that I hadn't split my love, but kept it all for my hoss, as it was in the beginning, is now, and ever will be as long as I live. That's what *I* should feel," repeated he, "that I hadn't split my love!"

Sunshine made a playful kick with the white heel, intimating the probable division of a certain body corporate, in the belief of the affection spoken of being other than a strict monopoly.

"If so be that I get fifty pounds a year, a cottage near a wood, and a missis to look after my linen, and make my gruel when a little off," repeated Puffy Doddles, " I'll have a bower with scarlet beans a-growin' and a-blowin' all over it, and there I'll sit of a summer's evening, and smoke my pipe, and ride the Leger over and over again, all by myself, and yet not alone, old feller, for you'll be always with me; as the song goes, 'though lost to sight, to memory dear.' "

Having heard, perhaps, enough upon the subject of himself,

Sunshine gave an irritable switch of his tail, which seemed to say, " Cut it short."

" Never could bear to wait for your feed, old feller, could ye ? " continued Robert Top's best lad. " *You* know the time o' day, and can tell it as well as an eight-day clock. A hoss like you has a better head than many Christian folk, and a precious deal better heart."

CHAPTER XV.

WITHIN a week of the great race being numbered with the past, one of the principal actors in that truly exciting scene was taking a stroll up in the morning early, and almost as soon as the lark began to think of shaking the dewdrops from his wings. Upon the open Downs, stretching away in the distance as far as the eye could reach, in hill and valley, ridge, slope, and undulated ground, and in the immediate vicinity of Sunshine's training quarters, Puffy Doddles was enjoying a walk for the combined purposes of keeping himself " light," and indulging in the hope that " early to bed and early to rise " might render him " healthy, wealthy, and wise."

" Good morning," was the salutation which fell upon his ear from—in military language—his extreme rear.

Robert Top's best lad wheeled—still to adopt the phraseology of the army—upon his heel, and there stood face to face to him a stranger.

From force of habit, Puffy Doddles repeated the stranger's common-place words, saying neither more nor less than " good morning."

" It's a very nice morning, sir, is it not ? " said the stranger, still sticking to the then state and condition of the morning.

Puffy Doddles thought there could be but one opinion concerning the then state and condition of the morning, and said so.

"If I don't lay myself open to be written down as thundering a fool as ever drew breath," continued the stranger, "or that my eyes oughtn't to be condemned for not being worth twopenn'orth of cat's-meat, I have the honour of speaking to the great Mister Doddles?"

"The great Mister Doddles!" O, Puffy! O, Robert Top's best lad! How those words tickled something beneath thy flannel waistcoat!

Puffy Doddles pressed two fingers upon his lips, and seemed to be suddenly afflicted with a dry, hacking cough.

"My name is Doddles," replied he, blushing like a peony; "Puffy Doddles; but as to—to—to being the great Mister Doddles——"

"And no other," interrupted the stranger. "You're the out-an'-out, tip-top swell of the Doddles. Didn't you win the Leger?"

"I rode the winner o' the Leger," was Puffy's modest reply.

"Ex-actly so," rejoined the stranger, with a look which may be described as a mixture of the "knowing" and "comical." "And he didn't try to run away with ye, did he?"

Robert Top's best lad started as if then subjected to the influence of a galvanic battery. His eyes, for the first time, scanned the stranger at a glance, and he saw that a short, thick-set man, whose round head, set upon a pair of broad shoulders, corpulent body, and slender, tightly-dressed legs gave him the appearance of a peg-top, was the promoter of the suggestion that no attempt had been made by Sunshine to run away with him in the great race before referred to. He also perceived that the peg-top figure possessed features which closely assimilated those belonging to a ferret, combined to a complexion coming under the denomination of pimply.

"I say," resumed the peg-top figure, "he didn't try to run away with ye?"

"Who said he did?" rejoined Puffy Doddles, in a gloomy, discontented tone and manner.

"No one but a sanguinary perverter of the truth could," returned the stranger. "A hoss like that might be ridden with packthread."

Puffy Doddles recollected, at this moment, one of the rudiments of his early education, to hold his tongue.

There was an awkward pause. The peg-top figure walked some yards, shoulder to shoulder, with Robert Top's best lad in silence, and kept watching the end of his large, square-toed boots, as they alternately preceded each other, giving his head the monotonous motion of a pendulum, swaying from one side to the other.

Puffy Doddles felt most uncomfortable, and wished himself anywhere else than shoulder to shoulder with the stranger.

"I dare say," observed the peg-top figure, breaking the most awkward silence that Robert Top's best lad ever experienced in the whole course of his stable existence, and continuing to examine his square-toed boots, "that you may have heard of my name, although we never met before ? "

Puffy Doddles might have done so, from those unforeseen and unexpected causes called accidents; but until learning the name by which the peg-top figure was designated from the common herd, it was next to impossible to arrive at any positive decision upon the point.

"My name is Sweety."

Puffy Doddles again started, and the shock of the galvanic battery was once more perceptible.

And there stood, or—for the description to be strictly in accordance with the fact—walked, minutely examining the ends of his toes, Sweety, he who "once got round a certain Matilda, the bit of muslin that nearly ruined all Yorkshire ! "

"I see that you've heard my name before," resumed the peg-top figure, "Job Sweety."

"Ye—es," drawled Robert Top's best lad, staring at Job Sweety's pimply countenance; "I heard it mentioned once."

"By George Spindles, I suppose ? " rejoined Job Sweety.

Puffy Doddles gave a brief affirmative in reply.

" I thought so," continued the peg-top figure; "and he didn't forget to couple with it a plump, pretty, little black-eyed lass of the name of Matilda, did he ? "

Robert Top's best lad thought this subject too delicate for discussion.

" Well, well ! " resumed Job Sweety, "perhaps it is, and so we won't say anything more about it. But George never forgave me for that Matilda cross. Ha ! ha ! ha ! Never forgave me for that Matilda cross ! " and then a laugh followed which may fitly be described as both long and loud.

Puffy Doddles feeling still more uncomfortable now that he knew who the peg-top figure was, announced his intention of leaving him to his solitude, and returning home.

" Wait a bit," returned Job Sweety. " We mustn't part so. We didn't meet by accident," continued he. " I've been watching for the last three days for an opportunity of speaking to you."

" What for ? " asked Puffy Doddles, with a gloomy brow and dissatisfied air.

" To be of benefit to each other," responded Job Sweety ; " and not like two swimming Irish pigs, the longer they swim, the more they cut their own throats. Now listen to me," he continued. ."That runaway dodge o' your stable gave me ' Jack up the orchard.' I as nearly went broke as a toucher, and it's nothing, therefore, but as natural for me to try and get some of my money back as it is for a cuckoo to suck small birds' eggs. You're in luck. I'm out of luck. That's the difference between you and I ; but you have learnt enough to know by this time that in racing, as it is, I suppose, in most things where money is to be made, it's every man for himself. People may talk about robberies ; but those who talk the most about being robbed are among the first to put their fingers in the nearest unbuttoned pocket. *I* don't complain of being robbed by your runaway dodge. My sorrow is that I wasn't in the swim, instead of being dropped in the hole. *I* don't complain of old Sloper, or you, or any one. It was a good game, well played, because successful. Everything in this world, Doddles—you'll excuse me for dropping the great Mister just now—is measured by the rule and compasses of success or failure. That which loses is the chalk ; that which pays is the cheese."

Puffy Doddles could not stop to listen to much more.

"In that case," resumed Job Sweety, "I'll come to the point at once. Your hoss's next engagement, the Grand Duke Michael Stakes, is a booked certainty for him. There is nothing in the race that can make him even gallop."

" That's just what I think," observed Robert Top's best lad, with a glow of pleasure illuminating his features.

" You'll have the mount, of course ? " rejoined Job Sweety.

" If I live and am well," returned Puffy Doddles, with marked confidence in the promise he had received that he should ride Sunshine in the remainder of his engagements, either made or to be made.

" It will be long odds on him," continued Job Sweety ; " but as most books will be closed against him, there can be but little betting. Sloper would make money out of the hoss, if he could, or what I should say, perhaps, dare ; but to make him safe this journey is more than old Sloper himself dare do. It would render his place too hot to live in, and this he knows as well as any one. Now, what I want is, to have one throw with the dice which old Sloper has often played with before; but which he can't load this time. Do ye understand, Doddles ? "

Puffy Doddles confessed that he did not quite understand, but should do so presently, perhaps.

" We're coming to the point by degrees, you see," said Job Sweety. "There's nothing like coming to the point by degrees. Now, suppose I was to lay you five hundred to nothing that Sunshine won the Grand Duke Michael Stakes, and he lost ; you'd have to take from me five hundred pounds, wouldn't ye ? "

Robert Top's best lad nodded his head gloomily.

"And if I forked out a clean hundred pound note," and as he spoke he suited the action to the words by producing from a pocket-book this easily transferrable security, "and handed a clean hundred pound Bank of England note to you, which I now do, the shutters, so to speak, of your understanding might begin to be taken down, perhaps, and the daylight to dawn like blazes!"

"Do you want me to pull him?" sharply inquired Puffy Doddles, crumpling the Bank of England note in the palm of a firmly clutched hand.

"Oh, no!" replied Job Sweety, fixing a look of admiration upon each of his square-toed boots in turn. "That might do for our grandfathers; but, with the strong glasses now in use, anybody can see when Captain Armstrong's in the saddle, and it always leads to ugly remarks, besides being clumsy, and out of date. No, no, Doddles; you shall not pull him, but, on the contrary, pop in whip and spur, and make as good a show of trying to win as anything in the race."

"Go on," sulkily remarked Robert Top's best lad; but diving, nevertheless, the hand containing the Bank of England note into the secret depths of a pocket of his drab knee-breeches.

"The point is nearly reached," continued Job Sweety, producing three horse beans, and holding them out in the middle of a hand for the closer inspection of Puffy Doddles.

"What are these?" asked Robert Top's best lad.

"Beans," replied Job Sweety.

"And what are they for?" inquired Puffy Doddles.

"Your hoss, Sunshine," rejoined Job Sweety; "to be given in three doses: one for the third morning before the race, one for the second morning before the race, and one on the morning of the race. That's all, Doddles. Three beans for your hoss, Sunshine."

"And what will they do?" asked Robert Top's best lad.

"Win your money," responded Job Sweety, "and lose him the race. That's all, Doddles."

"They won't hurt——"

"Not a hair of his body," interrupted Job Sweety. "I give you my word of honour"—and as he spoke, he clapped his broad, thick, right hand upon the left of his breast—" they won't hurt a hair of his body."

"Are they poison?" inquired Puffy Doddles, taking possession of the beans, and turning them over in his hand.

"Not exactly poison," returned Job Sweety. "A large quantity might polish off a hoss; but what I have given, if taken all at once, would only make him feel sick, faint, and off his feed for a few days."

"They won't hurt him, then?" said Puffy Doddles, pocketing the beans.

"I give you my word of honour," repeated Job Sweety, again slapping his broad, thick, right hand upon the left of his breast, "not a hair of his body."

"Very good," added Robert Top's best lad; and so saying, turned hurriedly, and quitted the spot.

"We understand each other, now?" hallooed Job Sweety.

Puffy Doddles waved a hand, without looking back, and they thus separated.

CHAPTER XVI.

MR. JAMES SLOPER had just completed the light task of chipping an egg, as a preliminary to render the contents of the shell part and parcel of an extremely good, albeit plain and substantial breakfast, when Robert Top's best lad signified a request for permission to enter the apartment by the loud application of his knuckles upon the panel of the door.

"Come in!" shouted Mr. James Sloper; and Puffy Doddles accordingly came in.

"Your servant, sir," said Robert Top's best lad, respectfully pulling the piece of hair sprouting luxuriantly upon his forehead.

"Oh, it's you, Doddles, is it?" returned Mr. James Sloper, as clearly and cheerfully as a piece of buttered toast, undergoing the process of mastication, permitted. "Oh, it's you, Doddles, is it?" repeated Mr. James Sloper.

"If you please, sir, it is," replied Puffy Doddles.

"Then I *do* please," rejoined Mr. James Sloper, in one of the most pleasant humours imaginable; "and therefore, there cannot be any doubt upon the point. What is it, Doddles, that makes you look rather pale this morning—not the willy-wabbles, I hope?"

"No, sir, thank you," replied Robert Top's best lad, placing a hand affectionately upon his abdominal regions; "it's all right here, sir."

"Glad to hear it," rejoined his employer. "Where is the screw loose, then?"

"They've been a-trying to get at me," returned Puffy Doddles, with an expression of deep melancholy; "to nobble me, sir."

"To nobble *you!*" repeated Mr. James Sloper, in a tone of great amazement, bordering on bewilderment.

"Well, sir," added Robert Top's best lad, dejectedly, "it's the same thing. They've been a-trying to buy me to nobble my hoss."

"Have they, indeed?" exclaimed Mr. James Sloper. "And who are *they* we've to thank for trying to get at you, Doddles?"

"Job Sweety," replied Sunshine's faithful attendant.

"Oh, indeed!" ejaculated Mr. James Sloper. "That thief, eh? Well, well! one good turn deserves another. Tell me all about it, Doddles."

Without omitting the smallest unimportant particular, Puffy Doddles narrated all that was said and done in the interview between himself and Job Sweety, and, in conclusion, placed the three horse-beans, with great precision, in a row upon the snow-white breakfast-cloth, and offered the hundred pound Bank of England note to Mr. James Sloper.

"No, no," said his employer; "keep that. You may find it useful."

"But I shan't do the job it was given me for," expostulated Puffy Doddles.

"A bean *is* a bean," replied Mr. James Sloper. "You agreed to give your hoss three beans. Very good. Then give him *those*," and as he spoke he produced three beans from a sample which he carried apparently in a deep waistcoat-pocket, "instead of *these*," pointing, at the same time, to the shells disguising the drug intended for making Sunshine safe. "You can't have any objection to do that, Doddles, for a hundred pound Bank of England note?"

"Oh, no, sir," responded Robert Top's best lad, "not at all."

"Then put that note into the exchequer," rejoined his employer, flipping the note playfully, with the end of his finger and thumb, towards Puffy Doddles. "Then put that into the exchequer," repeated he.

Thinking, at that moment, of the necessary expenditure for the contemplated cottage near a wood, and the bower of scarlet-beans, Puffy Doddles readily conformed to the instructions for putting the hundred pound Bank of England note into the exchequer, by pocketing it.

"Job Sweety will find himself again dropped in the hole," observed Mr. James Sloper, with a chuckle. "He has no one to thank this time but himself. It wouldn't surprise me to hear of his taking to dealing in lap-dogs again."

"Did he ever deal in lap-dorgs, sir?" asked Robert Top's best lad.

"That was Job Sweety's first business in life," replied Mr. James Sloper, smiling; "a dog-dealer, and, perhaps, we might

add, a dog—— Well! something that rhymes with dealer,
Doddles, which I'll leave you to guess."

"Such as him, sir," rejoined Puffy Doddles, "ought to stick
to dorgs. They're a disgrace to hosses."

"Well, well, Doddles!" returned Mr. James Sloper;
"somebody said—I forget who—that the Turf levels all above
it, as it does all beneath it; and neither you nor I have any
cause to complain, as yet, of the turf, let who will tread
upon it."

"That's true, sir," added Robert Top's best lad, reflectively;
"as true as boiled fleas an't lobsters."

"Ha, ha!" laughed Mr. James Sloper. "Quite so. Ha,
ha! As true as boiled fleas an't lobsters! I like that. As
you grow richer, Doddles," continued his employer, "you grow
smarter."

"I'm glad you think so, sir," was the reply of Robert Top's
best lad. "It wouldn't do for the Great——"

Puffy Doddles stopped short, and blushed with the hue of
a poppy.

"Go on," encouragingly said Mr. James Sloper. "Don't
stop at 'Great,' Doddles."

"It popped out, sir, unawares," responded Sunshine's attendant, now as red from chin to forehead, including his ears,
as a freshly-scraped carrot. "But——"

"Don't hesitate," remarked Mr. James Sloper, his curiosity
fairly roused to be made acquainted with the completion of the
sentence.

"But," resumed Robert Top's best lad, in stammering
accents, "I was going to call myself what Job Sweety called
me".

"And what was that?" inquired Mr. James Sloper.

"The Great Mister Doddles!"

"Did he, though!" exclaimed Mr. James Sloper. "I'm
glad you told me that," continued he. "Champagne and cigars
spoil a good many stable lads, and young jockeys; but they are

not half so bad as Buttered Gammon. Buttered Gammon, if swallowed in large quantities, and often, would poison the best lad—ay, even Robert Top's best lad."

The tips of the ears of Puffy Doddles glowed painfully at this moment.

"Beware of Buttered Gammon," said Mr. James Sloper, raising his forefinger, and bearing a fair resemblance to a lecturer upon ethics about to dwell upon a favourite subject, and with which he was well acquainted. "If you must swallow poison," continued he, in a voice approaching the solemn, still with the forefinger raised, "if something within says ' poison,' take one of these," and he pointed to a bean comprising a unit of the small stock supplied by Job Sweety, "in preference to a mouthful of Buttered Gammon. Women, kingdoms, worlds, and stable lads have been, are, and will be ruined with Buttered Gammon. Keep it at arm's length, Doddles. Keep it at arm's length," and, drawing his closed hand gently over his features, he slightly opened his fingers, aad took a peep between them at Puffy Doddles.

Robert Top's best lad not only felt inclined to shed a tear, but did so, from a feeling of gratitude that he had been saved from the poisonous effects of " Buttered Gammon."

***

CHAPTER XVII.

" Oh, that a man might know
The end of this day's business ere it come !
But it sufficeth that the day will end
And then the end is known."

THAT day arrived, towards the close of the racing season, on which the Grand Duke Michael Stakes formed the coveted prize for competition, and when the victor of the great double event was to be brought out—if the prophecies of all the prophets were to be fulfilled—to add to his high honours by cantering away easily from the small probable list of starters, and winning, if thought advisable, in that gentlest of all paces, known as a walk.

"What's to beat him?" inquired a small, light-figured man, dressed in a long pepper-and-salt coat, billy-cock hat, and a cravat of very loud colours. "What's to beat him?" repeated he, engaged in sucking the end of a silver-mounted, straight-cutting whip.

"Nothing," replied a member of the ring, who had formerly introduced himself to Robert Top's best lad as "Job Sweety."

"Bar accident," rejoined the proprietor of the whip, still sucking the silver knob, "and there's nothing to make the show of a race with him."

Now, be it known that these remarks were—as may readily be conjectured—anent the colt by Glitter, dam Comet, by Falling Star, and that they were made and delivered on that identical spot of Her Most Gracious Majesty Queen Victoria's dominions known as the Heath at Newmarket, at the precise moment when Puffy Doddles, in the weighing room, was turning the beam for the requisite weight to be carried in the Grand Duke Michael Stakes.

"They've laid ten to one on him," said Job Sweety, referring to a row of entries in his betting book.

"It's any odds on him," returned the possessor of the whip. "Bar accident."

"Or bar something else," deliberately interposed Job Sweety.

He of the whip—still sucking the end of the silver-mounted handle—glanced furtively at Job Sweety's dark, closely-set eyes, bearing the impression of a hawk with a good appetite, and about to make a fell swoop upon a brood of newly-fledged ducklings.

"I say," added Job Sweety, keeping his gaze fixed upon a page of the betting book, "or bar something else."

"You don't mean——"

“I mean this,” interrupted Job Sweety, suddenly closing his volume. “I mean that I have laid against the hoss until I dare not lay any more. It is said that I am about the only man who has laid any amount against him, and if I went on, I might be called upon to·cover, which wouldn't be so convenient as if I had Lombard Street at my back.”

The owner of the whip stood in an attitude denoting con-certrated attention.

“There's nothing, however, to prevent your executing a commission for me,” resumed Job Sweety.

“Nothing, so long as——”

“I pay if I lose, and receive if I win,” added Job Sweety, with impatience both in tone and manner. “Is that it?”

The proprietor of the whip nodded.

“Very good,” continued Job Sweety. “Will you take my word of honour that I shall pay any loss I may meet with on this race?”

“If——”

“I can show you the means of· paying,” interrupted Job Sweety.

The owner of the silver-mounted, straight-cutting whip nodded again, as an affirmative signal.

“The means of paying, then,” resumed Job Sweety, looking suspiciously over each of his shoulders, to see that no listener was near, “are, the hoss is made safe.”

The frame beneath the long pepper-and-salt coat seemed to have met with an unexpected blow in a most tender spot.

“Nobbled?”

“Nobbled!” echoed Job Sweety.

“The stable?” inquiringly said the owner of the whip.

“Is in the hole,” hoarsely whispered Job Sweety. “The lad was got at.”

“I'm to lay——”

“Don't stop laying,” interrupted Job Sweety, impatiently. “Go on as long as they'll back him for a quid.”

The commission having been sent out to lay against Sunshine to an unlimited extent, the two separated.

Saddled and mounted, the best judges present made no hesitation in declaring that Sunshine "never looked in finer fettle since he was first stripped for a race."

Job Sweety was among the select number congregated at the starting post, and he was seen to go close to the head of the horse, as he approached, with Puffy Doddles in the saddle, and peer with a searching gaze at the eyes of the favourite. The result seemed anything but satisfactory; for as he did so his face turned to a creamy white, and the pimples looked like spots of ink. With a brow, lowering with ill-disguised passion, he raised three fingers, bending at the same time a frowning and inquiring look upon the honest and gratified features of Robert Top's best lad, who responded to the signal by also raising three fingers of his whip‚hand.

Job Sweety was evidently puzzled. He again fixed a blinkless gaze upon Sunshine's eyes; but his face became several shades more yellow as he looked, and the pimples of an inkier tint.

"You sanguinary, juvenile appropriator!" muttered he, between his clenched and grating teeth. "You've done me!" continued he, in the same savage tone. "But look out! I'll have my revenge."

It was not improbable that Puffy Doddles remained ignorant of the threat, from the subdued tone in which it was uttered; for no effect was visible, as he turned Sunshine to take his position for the start, that he had heard the intention proclaimed of Job Sweety "having his revenge."

Mr. James Sloper watched the proceedings from a short distance, with great interest, and appeared never more satisfied with himself or mankind in general, than when he went to Sunshine's side for the purpose of giving Puffy Doddles his final orders.

"Did that thief speak to you?" inquired he.

"He said something, sir," replied Robert Top's best lad; "but I didn't hear exactly what."

"I saw him lift three fingers, telegraphing about the beans," observed Mr. James Sloper, laughing.

"Yes, sir, he did," rejoined Puffy Doddles, "and I thought I'd just lift three o' mine, as a sort of answer."

"Quite right," returned Mr. James Sloper. "I have heard of talking with the fingers. Why not chaff with them?"

As was anticipated, a small field appeared only as competitors for the Grand Duke Michael Stakes, and the whole of the several horses coming to the post had been "run through," either directly or indirectly, by Sunshine. No wonder, then, that the followers of the stable should look upon the anticipated result as a foregone conclusion. No wonder, then, that long odds should be laid upon Sunshine's winning, and scarcely less wonder, perhaps, that Mr. James Sloper should treat the race, in giving directions for the manner in which "the crack" was to be ridden, as "a certainty."

"Take the lead, make strong running, and——"

Puffy Doddles bent low, towards his near stirrup iron, to hear the finish of the sentence.

"Cut their throats," concluded Mr. James Sloper.

CHAPTER XVIII.

Sunshine supported the character he possessed of being "a good beginner," by jumping off with the lead, and making the running so strong that but a short distance of the one mile, two furlongs, and seventy-three yards, "Across the Flat," had been accomplished, when it was announced by stentorian lungs that "they would never catch him." On he skimmed like a fleet-winged swallow, making the distance wider, at every stride, between his haunches and the heads of his antagonists struggling in the rear. His rider, glancing behind him, saw the easy victory within his grasp, and a thought of what Job Sweety's feelings must be at that particular moment of the entry on the record of his mistakes and misdoings flashed through the memory of Puffy Doddles, and caused him to laugh in the sleeve of the wasp-like colours.

"I wonder what he thinks of the beans now?" said he, to his secret agent—himself. "I wonder what he would give not to have tried to get at *me?*"

On rushed the colt by Glitter, dam Comet, by Falling Star, already proclaimed the winner, with vociferous offers to "lay a hundred to one, or the Bank of England to a glass of gin that he won'in a walk."

No evidence exists, either by admission or otherwise, of Puffy Doddles having heard these proffered ventures for small gains at large risks; but no second opinion can possibly be entertained upon the fact that as Sunshine carried him, "like a bird," within a few lengths of the winning post, he pulled the horse up short to "walk in."

It might be a shaft winged by Fate; it might be that the brain of Robert Top's best lad had been turned, from circumstances of late, the wrong side uppermost; it might be that in looking over his shoulder on the off side, he did not perceive the stealthy approach of a single opponent on the near side; but, whatever the cause, "true it is, and pity 'tis 'tis true," this one horse, on the near side, caught him, and before Sunshine could be set going again, notwithstanding the most strenuous efforts on the part of his almost appalled rider, he was defeated on the post by "a short head."

Such was the fiat of the judge.

Within the memory of that imperishable antediluvian, "the oldest inhabitant," never was there such a "sensation" on the Heath at Newmarket. It could not be believed that Sunshine had been beaten by such a cur as "The Counterfeit," and a thousand questions were asked simultaneously concerning the how, and why, and wherefore. "Was it a robbery, a cross, a swindle, a do, or, if not, what was it, or how otherwise?" To state that Puffy Doddles was mobbed as ˉhe returned to scale ; to say that hisses, groans, and maledictions fell upon his ears on every side, would feebly convey the expression of public opinion against him. . Men appeared to vie with each other in giving vent to their anger. and disappointment, and ill, indeed, would it have fared with Robert Top's best lad had a tithe of the torments been inflicted which were suggested for his immediate punishment, for losing the Grand Duke Michael Stakes —the greatest certainty that was ever known.

"What have you to say for yourself?" asked Mr. James Sloper in a voice husky with passion, as Puffy Doddles dismounted with one of the most rueful visages ever possessed by a losing jockey, young or old.

Robert Top's best lad looked appealingly at his employer, but only shook his head with a sad and almost despairing gesture.

"What made you stop him on the post?" shouted Mr. James Sloper, with an expression of countenance closely assimilating to that of a cat caught between the iron teeth of a strong trap.

"I— I— I——" stammered Puffy Doddles ; but he could proceed no further.

"You what?" hissed his employer.

"Thought to win in a walk, sir," added Robert Top's best lad, bursting into a flood of tears which, from its violence, might come under the definition of "blubbering," and nothing less.

"Win in a walk!" sneered Mr. James Sloper, with a clenched fist itching to increase the tears now rolling fast, and as big as peas, down the cheeks of the broken-hearted Puffy Doddles. "Win in a walk!" repeated he. "Were not your orders to 'cut their throats?'"

"Well, sir!" expostulated Robert Top's best lad, and screwing a bent knuckle into the corner of each eye, "I—I— I thought I had cut their throats. I didn't see the beggar on the near side."

. Mr. James Sloper groaned in his agony. Here was the truth, and he felt it. Puffy Doddles had been caught napping, and the race had been stolen from him. Mr. James Sloper stamped a foot upon the ground, after the manner of an excited rabbit, and indulged in some muttered anti-scriptural phrase, adding, " What a pot to boil over ! "

Races won, however, are races done, and there was no cure, no remedy for the mistake committed. " The Ring," or, more properly speaking, those members belonging to the magic circle who had opened their books against Sunshine, expressed in loud demonstrations the unlimited extent of joy entertained at the unexpected defeat of Sunshine. Hats were thrown up wildly, cheer succeeded cheer, and a few danced like that popular Ethiopian known as " old Joe, kicking up behind and before." But if every medal and coin has its reverse, not more opposite than head is to tail were the feelings of Puffy Doddles to these noisy ebullitions of triumph.

Threading his way through the throng, and avoiding with downcast eyes the looks of fierce reproach bent upon him from every side, Robert Top's best lad walked slowly towards the town of Newmarket, and in every step taken felt that he, in his own person, was a funeral, following his coffined hopes and honours. Where was " the great Mister Puffy Doddles " now ? A fresh jet of tears burst forth and answered the " still small voice" within, and the bearer of that name, so lately proud of its distinction, felt that most willingly would he exchange it on the spot for that of a departed criminal.

CHAPTER XIX.

DARK, indeed, was the cloud which had lowered over the head of Puffy Doddles, and to which there appeared as yet no silver lining. His society, so far from being sought, and even courted by his superiors, equals, and inferiors, was avoided, without the smallest attempt being made to save appearances. The cut direct, and in its most positive form, was given to Robert Top's best lad. The hardest possible names were applied to him as descriptive of his attributes, and among them he frequently understood that he was held in the estimation of "a muff." To that depth, to which there appeared no lower, had Puffy Doddles sunk in the affections of his friends and admirers, that he often was informed that the only testimonial they were either ready or willing to present to him was a limited number of inches of hempen twist for the direct purpose of hanging himself. No one had a word to offer in extenuation for the error he had committed, and even his self-reproach, admission, confession, and penitence seemed in no way to mitigate the acrimony of his accusers. Not a thought was bestowed upon the perfection of jockeyship displayed by him in carrying the wasp-like colours to the front in the Great St. Leger, or the incessant care and heartfelt interest he took in the horse he loved almost to devotion. The fault alone was remembered. He had lost the Grand Duke Michael Stakes.

To-morrow, however, succeeded yesterday, in the well-timed order of the earth's revolutions upon her own axis, day followed day, and the omissions and commissions of others, erroneous, wise, and otherwise, began to engross attention. Time—the curer of all evils—lightened the load of Puffy's sorrows, and he even commenced the belief that he should reject the offer of exchanging his surname of Doddles with that of a departed criminal. When nobody was near, it may also be mentioned, as a proof that his spirits were again slightly in the ascendant, that he might be heard to whistle at his work, in a subdued tone, that favourite air, "Of all the girls that are so sweet," Sally being the heroine. In short, his fault of the past began to be forgotten in the fulness of time, and was more vividly remembered, perhaps, by himself, and with more bitter associations, than by the most unfortunate of Sunshine's supporters.

Puffy Doddles felt that the one fault of his life—"not seeing the beggar on the near side"—would be the skeleton at the feast, and the dark closet in his household, for long, and it might be for ever. With much less despondency, however, he now regarded this terrible misfortune, and trusted generally in the hope of having "better luck next time."

While brushing lightly, tenderly, but, at the same time, efficiently, the white heel of the Colt by Glitter, dam Comet, by Falling Star, one autumnal morning, Puffy Doddles heard a short cough given, by way of calling his attention, as it seemed, to the promoter, and as he paused in his task, and glanced upwards, he saw that he was in the presence of Mr. James Sloper.

As was his wont, Robert Top's best lad exhibited his careful training in politeness by a bow of the best to his superior.

Mr. James Sloper made no sign of being sensible of the politeness; but stood sternly watching Puffy Doddles, as he resumed the work of brushing Sunshine's white heel.

Mr. James Sloper coughed a second time, but spoke not a word.

The silence proved extremely trying to Puffy Doddles, feeling, as he did, that it was only a calm preceding, what he most thoroughly feared, a gale of no gentle description.

At length, and when the nerves of Puffy Doddles were wrought to a pitch of insufferable acuteness, Mr. James Sloper coughed a third time, and thus began—

" I have something to say to *you*, my young friend."

Every pore in the skin of Robert Top's best lad opened at these words, delivered, as they were, in a tone and manner expressive of anything but a friendly nature, and he felt cold drops ooze out, and, blending together, run down in icy streams from various parts of his body.

Mr. James Sloper perceived the impression the opening of his address had made, and was determined to follow up the advantage by slowly, deliberately, and emphatically repeating his words, " I have something to say to *you*, my young friend."

The ears of Puffy Doddles appeared to prick forward to catch the succeeding syllable, and he stood mute with his lower jaw dropped, an illustration of marked attentiveness.

"If," resumed his employer, "I had served you out as I was recommended, after that pretty bit o' business of yours, I should have kicked ye out of my stable without a character, or *with* the character of not obeying orders.   Whichever you pleased."

Puffy Doddles, even at this early stage of the proceedings, had to cut off certain springs, which began to rise, and threatened to dim his vision.

"You would then," continued Mr. James Sloper, "in all probability, have never got into another training stable, and must have taken to scaring rooks, grinding a mangle, or"—here his employer made a most effective pause—"turned gardener, perhaps, to an old maiden lady.   Think of turning gardener, Doddles, to an old maiden lady!"

At this sad picture, Puffy Doddles could not restrain a whimper.

"Taking that pity upon ye," said Mr. James Sloper, "which others wouldn't, I did *not* kick ye out of my stable."

Robert Top's best lad felt, at this juncture, what a debt of gratitude he owed for not being subjected to the summary mode of ejectment referred to by his employer.

"Such being the case," continued Mr. James Sloper, "and no fault being found with ye since—we won't be particular as to when—I have almost made up my mind to give ye another chance."

Puffy Doddles gasped with expectation.

"I may be called a fool," said his employer, "and, I dare say, shall be ; but I have almost made up my mind to give ye another chance."

Puffy Doddles ventured to offer up a little secret prayer that Mr. James Sloper's mind might be relieved from all doubt, with all practicable expedition.

"Now, if I *do* give ye another chance," resumed his employer, "I suppose I can depend upon you, this time, riding to orders?"

Robert Top's best lad was about making most violent protestations of strictly complying with the instructions he might receive, when he was stopped from uttering a word by the raised forefinger of the right hand of Mr. James Sloper.

"I know what you would say," continued he; "but I don't care the value of that"—and, as he spoke, he stooped and picked up a single straw which laid at his feet—"what anybody says. Words won't either make or break me. It's what you do, Doddles, or don't do, that concerns me."

Finding it useless to speak, Puffy Doddles exercised a wise discretion by observing a strict silence.

"In the belief, then," said Mr. James Sloper, "that you will make no more attempts to 'walk in'—— "

The two last monosyllables, pointedly directed, entered poor Puffy's bosom in the shape of a couple of barbed fish-hooks.

"I've almost made up my mind," continued he, "to give ye another chance."

"Oh, that he would give the particulars of the chance!" was the mental exclamation of Puffy Doddles.

"They think they've stopped him," said Mr. James Sloper; but the remark appeared to be designed as part of a soliloquy rather than for the information of Robert Top's best lad. "They think they've stopped him," repeated he, with a jerk of the head at the Invisible and Airy Nothing, taking up its temporary quarters in a corner of Sunshine's box; "but they haven't. Top weight as he is, eight stone seven won't stop him, and, if he runs kindly, he'll be there or thereabouts."

What can describe the feverish anxiety of Puffy Doddles to learn the full details of the "there or thereabouts" to which direct reference was being made by his employer?

" He's a *race'*oss !" ejaculated Mr. James Sloper. " He can both stay and fly ! "

A sincere response was given to this sentiment by Puffy Doddles uttering a hearty " That he can ! "

Mr. James Sloper appeared, figuratively speaking, to be recalled to his senses, and to pass a hasty resolution upon the spot to confine his thoughts, instead of permitting them to range by " thinking aloud."

" You'll ride strictly to orders ? " interrogatively said he.

Puffy Doddles was about delivering an emphatic answer, when the raised forefinger again checked the words, until they died away in silence upon his lips.

" That being so," resumed Mr. James Sloper, " I have almost made up my mind to give ye another chance," and, upon completion of the sentence, abruptly quitted the box, leaving Robert Top's best lad to meditations both deep and painful.

CHAPTER XX.

THE racing season was drawing to a close. But one more great handicap had to be contended for previous to the commencement of the Houghton Meeting, in which Sunshine occupied the conspicuous place of " top weight." " The race being in the scales," it was the unanimous opinion of " the talent" that, good as Sunshine had proved himself to be, and great as his performances unquestionably were, it was not in his power " to pull off the Cesarewitch with eight stone seven." In other words, he was considered stopped by the weight. Books, therefore, were opened freely against the winner of the Derby and Leger, and book-makers snapped up stray offers to back him at " liberal odds," thirty to one being taken. It was soon. discovered that " the stable" had backed the horse for an. immense stake, and rumours of a favourable trial, in which it was declared that "he had cleared out the lot," soon shortened the "liberal odds ;" and, to the infinite surprise of "the talent," to say little of the profound astonishment of many not claiming to be associates of that distinguished body, the voice of the people (of Newmarket) began to declare that "it *was* in Sunshine's power to pull off the Cesarewitch with eight stone seven."

By degrees, as may be surmised, the chance of the colt by Glitter, dam Comet, by Falling Star, began to attain a lofty position, and the "top weight' in the handicap eventually occupied the first place in the betting.

Mr. James Sloper once more "stood on velvet," and the soft, smooth fabric appeared to agree remarkably well, meta-phorically speaking, with his feet. He had backed the horse at thirty to one, and a strong desire being manifested to "get out" by those who had fully opened their books against him, Sunshine stood firmly, on the morning of the race, at the short figure of six to one, as the "official report" added, taken.

By commission Mr. James Sloper, who never, either by word or sign, signified personally his intended operations in "the ring," edged his money, and found himself, some hours before the start, in that most pleasant and easy condition for a speculator on the turf, a probable winner of a good stake, and an impossible loser of nothing. Mr. James Sloper, therefore, "stood on velvet."'

Superfluous may it seem to state that, on the day appointed for the decision of the Cesarewitch, Newmarket was in that state commonly called "a bustle." Newmarket responded to the summons to "wake up" by "looking alive," and had shaken off that dead, calm, sepulchral appearance which gives to the stranger a superstitious dread of walking in her highways and byeways by moonlight. Ghosts, and things of the small hours which dance and revel when the stars glitter, may readily be pictured to have made Newmarket their head-quarters and general basis of operations. Nothing but "a great event" stirs up Newmarket, which, as a custom of ancient origin, seems to be indulging in a slumber of profound depth, and dreams of grandeur faded and by the world forgotten.

Periodically as Newmarket is "stirred up," be it remembered, nothing but "business" produces the sensation. No vulgar episodes are permitted (by the laws of custom) to be introduced in the race meetings of Newmarket. Pigeon pies are unknown. Lobster salads are as rarely to be seen upon the Heath as the English bustard, and the lively popping of champagne corks is a sound that is seldom heard. Odds "offered" and odds "taken," with "a card of the races," are words as familiar as any of the most common of household upon the Heath of Newmarket; but anything more would be deemed an infringement upon a recognised prerogative. The sayings and doings of Newmarket are confined to business.

And so the "muff" was to have the mount on the "crack" for the Cesarewitch, was he? Such was the intelligence, conveyed with great dispatch, and in some instances breathless speed, by "the post-horse Rumour." Puffy Doddles would wear the yellow and black—the wasp-like colours—upon this momentous occasion, and opinions differed concerning the expediency of the measure. Was a "muff" to be trusted to get through a great field of horses like the Cesarewitch? Wouldn't he be shut in? Hadn't he thrown away a race before, and wasn't it likely he'd do so again? Why not put a jockey up instead of a stable lad? Such were the questions asked by those inimically disposed towards Robert Top's best lad, and no more complimentary were put even by his affectionate friends, assuming that he possessed any, which appears doubtful.

Once more arrayed in the yellow and black, and mounted upon Sunshine, Puffy Doddles, it must be confessed, exhibited an appearance of combined vanity and ambition, with a tendency to the effect of being sole and arbitrary "monarch of all he surveyed." With something like disdain his upper lip curled as he criticised each horse approaching the starting-post, and in "taking stock" of the rival candidates, now drawn together in a compact body, he arrived at the somewhat hasty conclusion that "he should beat them all."

As the official report declared, "in consequence of the breaking away of several horses, a great deal of time was cut to waste in the endeavour to obtain a level start. At length, however, the praiseworthy efforts of the official were crowned with the most unequivocal success. The flag was lowered to one of the fairest starts ever seen." No ground of complaint, therefore, could exist of being left at the post either by design or accident.

The "good beginner" again supported the character he possessed of commencing well. Among the first off, Sunshine was seen to carry his colours to the front, occupying, however, that conspicuous position only for a space of time known as a "twinkling." Riding with a strictness to orders which could not be surpassed in the minutest detail, Puffy Doddles pulled his ardent horse back, remembering, with an impression not readily effaced, the emphatic words spoken by Mr. James Sloper just before having "a leg up," that "he was to wait, and come only at the finish."

Rather more than two-thirds of the two miles, two furlongs, and twenty-eight yards had been accomplished, when the field grew "smaller by degrees and beautifully less." A dozen horses at least, however, were still bearing away in front of Sunshine, who threatened to pull his rider clean out of the saddle unless an immediate compromise was made by being permitted to go nearer the leaders. An interval of a few seconds, and it became patent to all the watchers of the race that Sunshine was going up to the horses in front, and that they must make the pace better without the delay of a moment, unless resigned to the approaching result of being caught.

"Sunshine is with them!" cried a voice.

"What against Sunshine?" hallooed a second.

"I'll lay an even hundred that I name the winner," shouted a third.

"Sunshine wins!" was proclaimed by a hundred tongues, not one of which, however, produced the smallest perceptible effect upon the stoicism of Puffy Doddles. He was "riding to orders," and to orders only would he ride.

A single horse only now remained in front. Inch by inch Sunshine gained upon him, but it looked, as the two raced together, that Puffy Doddles came too late at the finish. With "hands down," and sitting as motionless as if carved from stone, he seemed to be again throwing a race away; but when upon the post itself, excruciatingly close for a nervous supporter of the "top weight," he was seen to call upon his horse to make his effort. Upon the post itself no visible space separated the two. Locked together they raced, and when barely sufficient ground remained for three strides to be taken, Puffy Doddles buried the rowels of his spurs deeply in Sunshine's flanks, and, as the "official report" declared, "amidst a scene of the wildest excitement, won the finest race that it has ever been our lot to witness."

As Robert Top's best lad dismounted to "weigh in," he was seen to examine the sides of his horse with anxious solicitude, and upon perceiving a crimson stream trickling from them, might have been observed to rub the end of his nose vigorously with the back of his whip hand.

A little more pressure upon his nervous system, and Puffy Doddles would have been more demonstrative in his grief for having given pain to his favourite.

CHAPTER XXI.

IN a neighbourhood of the metropolis so confined that the
smoke never effected an escape, and the fresh air was never
known to enter, a small hostelry was known by the name of
"Paddy's Goose." The frequenters and patrons of this small
hostelry bore the reputation of possessing the most limited
ideas concerning the rights of property; and looking back,
perhaps, to those good old times with veneration, when feudal
rights were founded on moral wrongs, carried out the principle of "taking" when the opportunity presented itself, and
"keeping" whatever fell into their hands. As with a veil
of the dirtiest kind, a yellow fog, sending forth a scent of
anything but "roses tipped with morning dew," dimly concealed, but did not hide, the surrounding charms of "Paddy's
Goose." The orange peel and oyster shells, alternately ob-
structing the inky and sluggish stream crawling like an idle
leech before the door, appeared to possess resources which
may be described as inexhaustible. The supply was always
more than equal to the demand : hence the great accumulation
of both. A gas lamp flared above the portal, making the
surrounding darkness, if anything, more visible, and light, air,
and space seemed, in the immediate vicinity of "Paddy's
Goose," to be condensed to homœopathic quantities.

Within, as without, the small hostelry was dingy in the
extreme. In the best parlour—an apartment measuring six
feet by four—the fog had evidently fraternised with some
fine, old, stale tobacco smoke, strongly flavoured with sour
beer. Upon the walls were suspended faded and fly-spotted
illustrations of "The Dog Billy" performing his wonderful
match ; "The Putney Pet, champion of the Heavy Weights ;"
"Bos Podgers, champion of the Middle Weights ;" "Spider
Jack, champion of the Light Weights," and other celebrities

of a similar description, as they severally appeared, stripped and ready for the fray.

The furniture consisted of two wooden chairs and a small table, the design being, apparently, that more than two were not expected to be present in the best parlour of "Paddy's Goose" at the same time. At the precise moment to which reference is being made it contained but one occupant—Job Sweety.

Whatever might be the virtues and vices of Job Sweety, either admitted or denied, patience could not be classed among the former. "He hated," as he frequently declared, with a large number of adjectives thrown in, to express more forcibly the warmth of his feelings, "to wait for any one or anything." Nothing gave Job Sweety more acute annoyance than to wait, it mattered not for whom or what. Now, it so occurred, in the disposition of events generally, that Job Sweety had been kept waiting in the best parlour of "Paddy's Goose" for a considerable time, in anticipation of the momentary advent of somebody whom he continued to describe in muttered language of the most uncomplimentary nature. When, however, his excited feelings led him to square his clenched fists at the portrait of "Bos Podgers, champion of the Middle Weights," and to throw himself in an attitude adapted alike for offence and defence, an approaching footstep was heard, and it must have been clear to all but the deafest of ears that "Somebody" was coming.

Job Sweety dropped his hands and arms, and stood with a scowling expression of countenance, denoting expectation of the immediate advent of "Somebody."

The door of the best parlour was thrown noisily back upon its hinges, and there stood "Somebody."

"Oh, you're come at last, eh?" growled Job Sweety, throwing himself down upon one of the wooden chairs, and crossing a leg, dexterously, but most impolitely, presented the broad of his back to "Somebody."

Yes, "Somebody" had come. What then?

"Might have come before and not kept a cove——"

"You be blow'd!" interrupted "Somebody."

As no more convenient opportunity may present itself for sketching the full-length portrait of "Somebody," the cartoon shall be drawn as he stands framed by the doorposts of the best parlour, and hesitating, as it would seem, whether to advance or retreat.

A big, burly fellow was "Somebody," with a head which, in shape and other properties, looked exceedingly like a bullet of more than ordinary size and thickness. A level fringe of black, straight hair hid whatever there might be of a forehead, and a remarkably short, muscular neck, much exposed to view from the negligent form in which the blue and white bird's-eye cravat was twisted round, gave an effect of decided animal tendency, rather than of an intellectual nature. High cheek bones, small, sunken, restless black eyes, a nose never handsome, perhaps, though anything but improved from the bridge being fractured in other days, and left to set as flat as a muffin, with a pair of thick, protruding lips, formed the irregular features making up the entire countenance of "Somebody." If arrayed in what is generally termed "his best," the state of his wardrobe was anything but satisfactory, consisting, as it did, of a greasy cloth cap, flannel jacket—anything but familiar with soap and water—knee breeches—spotted by too many solids and fluids for their colour to be perfectly described—and a pair of "ancle jacks." Such was the costume of "Somebody" as he stood framed by the door-posts of the best parlour of "Paddy's Goose."

"Why don't ye come in?" surlily inquired Job Sweety, glancing over his left shoulder.

"Why don't I come in?" repeated "Somebody," with a sneer. "'Cause I don't seem to be the party as is wanted."

"Come in, and don't make"— here Job Sweety intro- duced a powerful adjective—"a fool of yourself. I've been kept a-waiting"—another adjective here— "long enough."

"Have ye, though?" rejoined "Somebody," striding forward, and, pulling the unoccupied chair backwards between his legs, dropped upon the seat, and, stretching his feet out, with the heels resting upon the floor, seemed to settle himself in a position of great ease, if not of elegance.

"Well?" exclaimed Job Sweety, now turning round and facing his companion.

"Well?" repeated "Somebody," in a tone and manner clearly intended as an imitation of the original.

"You're a pretty kind of image, *you* are!" ejaculated Job Sweety, measuring "Somebody" with a slow look which, commencing with the "ancle jacks," terminated at the cerebrum.

"You're another!" complimentarily rejoined "Somebody."

"Come, cut this short," returned Job, with increasing ill-humour. "If you've got anything to say, say it, and don't let's have any more of this"—an adjective— "nonsense."

"If I've got anything to say," returned "Somebody," "I'm to say it, am I? Them's my orders, are they? Ho, indeed! Well, then, having a-something to say, here goes. Shall I shut the door first?"

Job Sweety nodded assent.

"Somebody" rose, and, after closing the door, occupied his seat in his former position, and thus began :—

"If ever there was one more ungrateful warmint on this bless-ed earth greater than another, you're that warmint. I'm a rogue. I was bred, born, and shall die a rogue; but for an out-an'-out thief, I don't know your equal, Job, and can't hope to live long enough to make his acquaintance."

"Cut it short!" growled Job Sweety.

"Cut it short, eh?" returned "Somebody." "Then short it is. Well then, as I was going to say, for an out-an'-out ——"

"You said that," interrupted Job Sweety.

"Did I? Ha, so I did," responded "Somebody," vigorously scratching the back of his head. "Well then, after what I've been and gone and done for you, Job, to treat a cove no better than a badger when he comes to see ye! I wonder you don't feel ashamed o' yourself!"

"I do," returned Job Sweety, with a short laugh.

"Supposin' I have kept ye waitin'," continued "Somebody," resuming the thread of his address without noticing the admission of his companion, "I've been kept waitin' whole days and nights about your precious business, without so much as pulling off my boots."

"Have ye done it?" inquired Job Sweety, harshly.

"Have I done it?" repeated "Somebody," drawing down the angles of his mouth. "Yes, I *have* done it;" and as he spoke he pulled a large key from one of the pockets of his flannel jacket, and held it up in triumph above his head.

"How did you manage it?" asked Job Sweety, fixing his eyes upon the key, as if to dispel any lurking doubt concerning its reality.

"How did I manage it?" returned "Somebody," who appeared to have a fixed habit of repeating whatever words were addressed to him. "Why, I managed it in my own way. Here's the key—where's my reg'lars?"

"Don't be short-tempered," expostulated Job Sweety, proceeding to count and place fifty sovereigns upon the table. "There's your reg'lars, Cupid."

Cupid looked much soothed at this prompt action on the part of Job Sweety, and a great improvement took place at once in his temper and general demeanour.

"You want to know how I managed it," said he, with a smile which showed he possessed only a few back teeth in his jaws. "You want to know how I managed it," repeated he, taking up the money, and placing it carefully in a canvas bag. "Well, then, it was in this way. I watched like a cat at a mouse-hole for a chance. The chance seemed as if it would never come; but come it did, as most chances will, if only waited long enough for. Once within a week"—Cupid here dropped his voice to a hoarse whisper—"I saw the key in the door, and no one on the outside. Quicker than I can tell ye, I whipped out a piece of moist clay, which I always carried in my pocket, and there was ——"

"The mark of the key itself," added Job Sweety, impatiently.

"Exactly so," continued Cupid, "and the key back in the lock, and no one a morsel the wiser."

"You're a clever fellow!" exclaimed Job Sweety. "The rest I can guess," continued he. "You got an old key ——"

"Filed and scoured it," said Cupid, taking up the thread of his narrative, "and the original one won't open the door easier. That I know, from having tried it."

"Well done, and done well!" ejaculated Job Sweety, and possessing himself of the key, he took an abrupt leave of Cupid, and was soon far from the precincts of "Paddy's Goose."

CHAPTER XXII.

UPON a dark and starless night, when the wind moaned through the trees, already wearing the decayed and decaying tints of approaching winter, a man crept, with stealthy tread, towards the door of a certain stable in Newmarket. With back inclined, and pausing at each step to listen with suspicious dread, his movements betokened a mind but ill at ease. It was Job Sweety preparing to accomplish one of the blackest deeds of his anything but spotless existence.

With a freedom which is sometimes accorded to the historian, the particular cause shall now be divulged of Job Sweety creeping, with stealthy tread, towards the door of a certain stable in Newmarket, to gain which he had now but to make some half-dozen strides.

Greatly to his own astonishment, and contrary to his final expectations, in the result of the race, he found himself a large winner upon the Grand Duke Michael Stakes, when Puffy

Doddles, in the display of too much confidence, essayed an un-successful attempt to win the race "in a walk." Much of the money he had lost formerly, when Sunshine was sent back in the betting through the "runaway dodge," was recovered, although correctly assigning the cause to be "a fluke." Among, however, a great number of "the talent" who held an opinion that Sunshine's chance in the Cesarewitch must be "stopped by the weight," was Job Sweety, and he resolved to "pepper" the colt by Glitter, dam Comet, by Falling Star. The unsatisfactory effect of the "peppering" need not further be alluded to, than to state simply that Job Sweety lost his money, and he again found himself—to use his own graphic description—"on the shady side of the hedge."

In the forthcoming handicap, the Cambridgeshire, in which Sunshine once more appeared as the "top weight," "the talent" arrived at a totally opposite opinion to that expressed on the Cesarewitch, concerning his power to "pull through." A unanimous opinion prevailed among "the talent" that, not-withstanding his increased weight, he had run so fast to the Bushes in the Cesarewitch that, in the shorter course, nothing could be anticipated to live with him at the finish. So thought "the talent," and the effect of the expression of the thought was that the public made "a rush" to "get on" Sunshine.

It was now, therefore, that Job Sweety determined to play a certain winning game with the favourite for the Cambridge-shire, holding the cards in his own hands, and trusting, this time, to the skill of no one but his own. All that he could lay, or get laid for him by commission, against Sunshine, had been booked, and on the eve of the last great race for the season he 'approached Sunshine's stable with a key which, if Cupid had not proved false to his trust, would give him ready admit-tance.

Hist ! What sound was that ?

It was only the beating of his heart, which thumped more loudly than its wont from craven fear. For if Job Sweety ever felt that to be a wretch, bent on wretched work, was to be most wretched, then, indeed, that moment had arrived when he noiselessly inserted the key into the lock of Sunshine's stable-door. A slight grating sound, as he slowly turned it, brought beads of perspiration upon his upper lip, and he stood on the threshold with wavering resolution whether to advance a single step or not. The thought, however, of what might be lost, and must be won, determined the course. He stole through the doorway like a shadow, and stood, as he conjectured—for the darkness was thick and impenetrable—within a few feet of the whereabouts of Sunshine.

Having been furnished by Cupid with a box of silent matches—similar to those used by the patrons of "Paddy's Goose" when engaged in certain nocturnal excursions—he struck a light, and, holding it above his-head, glanced with shrinking look around, as if apprehensive of detection from some quarter, and seemed to experience much relief at discovering no immediate cause for the rascal's prevailing fear—unmingled with compunction—of being "found out."

' The silent match threw a flickering, uncertain light upon the interior of Sunshine's stable; but enough could be seen, among the long fantastic shades and shadows cast around, to reveal the form of "the best of his year" standing in his stall prepared and "set" for the next day's struggle, the shrill crow of a watchful cock giving evidence of its advent.

Job Sweety struck a second silent match, upon which Sunshine turned his head, and, with pricked ears, watched the approach of the stranger with glaring eyes and distended nostrils.

His hand shook as if stricken with the palsy; but raising a heavy wooden mallet, which he drew from some secret part of his dress, Job Sweety struck the near hind leg of the horse sharply below the hock, and, as may be seen when a jaded bullock is hit in a similar way by a drover's goad, the limb was paralysed in a moment, and jerking it from the ground, he stood in trembling anguish, "nobbled" for the Cambridgeshire.

The work accomplished, Job Sweety hurried from the spot, carefully closing and locking Sunshine's stable door.

CHAPTER XXIII.

SUNSHINE'S career on the turf was closed. The last triumph had been recorded. "The best of his year" was doomed never to run again.

Useless would it be to dwell, however briefly, upon the disappointment and chagrin bitterly expressed by the multitude who had supported the pretensions of the "top weight" in the Cambridgeshire to add another green leaf to his laurels. He had been "made safe," and the absorbing question for a limited space in the history of man's misdoings was, "Who had rendered him so?" Criminations and recriminations were made and exchanged with the utmost freedom of speech. "The stable" was suspected. By turns the owner, trainer, head lad, and boys employed in and about the stable, individually and collectively, were suspected. No one having access, either direct or indirect, to the stable, but what came in for a full and liberal share of being suspected. Protests were made in vain. Conclusive proofs were offered that "the stable," having backed the "top weight" for a great stake, ought not to be suspected. The public had been robbed, and the public resolved that "some one" should be held responsible, if, individually, "no one" could be selected in particular. The "official report" came out upon the occasion, in language not only strong and vigorous, but violent. "A bare-faced, impudent, and cruel robbery had been effected," so said the official report, "and the matter should be sifted to the bottom."

It would appear, however, that the sifting to the bottom

produced no more profitable result than the sifting of the top. As in similar "robberies," the losers paid, the winners received ; and but few additional items in the earthly record of births, deaths, and marriages had been made, before the "nobbling" of Sunshine for the Cambridgeshire gave place for a "fresh sensation on the turf;" profitable and pleasurable to some, profitless and painful to others.

Robert Top's best lad had not one word to say on the subject, beyond announcing the simple, incontestable fact, that "in the morning early he found his horse lame in the near hind leg. That's all he knew. That's all he had to say." In speaking so little, perhaps, he thought the more ; but whatever might be his reflections, he kept them a secret never to be revealed, and was seen for days, and weeks, and months walking about alone, with his hands buried to the elbows in the pockets of his drab knee-breeches, staring at the ground, and evincing a strong tendency in his general demeanour of having "come to grief."

Sunshine's career on the turf was closed. Sanguine hopes, however, prevailed of "rosy hue," that Sunshine might become the parent of Sunbeams, bright, and beautiful, and true as their sire. With honours which few had won, the colt by Glitter, dam Comet, by Falling Star, retired, and Newmarket herself proclaimed, that "since a racehorse was first stripped, a better never looked through a bridle."

Time rolled on, and Puffy Doddles resumed, in increasing years, the figure of his youth. Robert Top's best lad became fat. An arch, or bow, was perceptible in that part of his body which physic and exercise had kept concave, and a "double chin" combined to show, by way of conclusive proof, that he no longer rode "sweating gallops," trials, or races. With Sunshine he, too, retired from the turf, notwithstanding tempting offers were made for him to continue to ride for the Great Stable of the North. Puffy Doddles had but one wish, "to look after Sunshine." This first desire of his heart was gratified, and in an arbour, with scarlet-beans growing and climbing luxuriantly over it, he may yet be seen, the freeholder of a cottage adjacent to a plantation, sitting, of a summer's night, smoking his pipe, and riding the Leger o'er and o'er again. A Mistress Doddles—of healthful and ruddy complexion, blue-eyed and comely—"looks after his linen, and makes his gruel when a little off;" but if pressed closely upon the point declares that "his love was never split."

FINIS.

FETTER AND GALPIN, BELLE SAUVAGE PRINTING WORKS, LUDGATE HILL, E.C.

field, and in an autumn, with scarlet-beans growing and climbing luxuriantly over it, he may yet be seen, the freeholder of a cottage adjacent to a plantation, sitting, of a summer's night, smoking his pipe, and riding the Leger o'er and o'er again. A Mistress Doddles—of healthful and ruddy complexion, blue-eyed and comely—"looks after his linen, and makes his gruel when a little off;" but if pressed closely upon the point declares that "his love was never split."

CPSIA information can be obtained
at www.ICGtesting.com
Printed in the USA
BVHW041103211218
536078BV00026B/275/P